To Natha

Best wishes

SOULKEEPERS

Steve Dean

Steve Dean.

ISBN 0-9550314-2-7

Cover art by Paul Cox

Cover layout by Garry Charles

Cover design by yo-yo.com, York

Prepared and printed by:
York Publishing Services Ltd
64 Hallfield Road
Layerthorpe
York
YO31 7ZQ
Tel: 01904 431213   Website: www.yps-publishing.co.uk

*This book is dedicated with love to my children;
Gary, Kim and Scott, who, despite having me as
a father, have turned out really quite well.*

Acknowledgements

The words in this book are all my own, but the book itself is the product of a great team.

Many thanks are due to Garry Charles, a great bloke and a man of infinite good taste and sharp eyes who brought this work to the publisher's attention. I owe him a debt I will probably never be able to repay.

Thanks also to the wonderful Hadesgate Crew:
Paula Wilson-Buckle, an organiser of Olympic standard, and David Pearce, a man with such depth of character he should be 15 feet tall.

Prologue

A cowled figure rode quietly across a wooded landscape.
The first rays of the dawn lit the sky with a soft white glow.
After a few miles the man came to a fork in the road.
Without slowing he guided his horse along the left branch.
The man knew these roads very well, having travelled them
for many years. Although the road was dim and many trees
formed dark shadows along both sides, neither the man nor
the horse showed any signs of fear.

Several miles later he came in sight of a small village to
one side of the road. Even at this early hour the villagers
were at work, rising with the sun to tend fields and livestock.
Although every person he passed looked towards him, none
spoke, none returned his warm smile. Halfway down the
main street, he turned into a narrow alley, heading for a
small house that formed the end of it. On the doorstep stood
a portly man, tall, with a rosy cheeked glow to his tanned
face.

"Good morning, Brother" said the man mechanically,
"She's in here." He stepped into the house to lead the way.

Brother Irator replied cheerily, "Good morning sir, all
is well I trust?"

The man stopped, turned round and said slowly "Yes
Brother," then carried on up the stairs and into a small
room. A bed took up most of the space. In the bed lay a
woman of similar appearance to the man, nursing a new-
born baby.

"If you could just lay her down here at the end of the
bed, then I can work better." Brother Irator smiled at the
woman, who merely did as she was ordered.

The baby began to cry as Irator opened out the rough
blanket to leave her naked and shivering in the cold of the
early spring day. The parents watched motionless as Irator

removed a clay jar, some herbs, a vial of yellow liquid, a thick oiled cloth and a small iron bowl from his pack. He placed the clay jar at the head of the squalling infant and removed the top. Next he poured the liquid into the bowl and added the herbs, which began to smoulder. Irator placed the bowl between the feet of the baby who cried louder at the cold touch. The Brother knelt down at the foot of the bed with his feet out of the door. A prayer of archaic origin began to issue from his mouth. The prayer grew faster, more complex, his hands wove a net of symbols in the air above the girl.

The atmosphere in the tiny room became suffocating. A strange thickness, almost a taste, filled every space, every corner, until the thin walls threatened to burst outwards. The air around the little child began to shimmer, as though great heat welled up from her skin. The shimmering gathered into a child shaped cloud that pulsed and drifted towards the clay jar. The Brother ended the prayer with a loud clap, causing the cloud to roll up and shoot into the jar. The baby screamed once then fell silent. With lightning speed Brother Irator grabbed the lid and slammed it shut. He took the cloth and bound it tightly around the top, forming a seal. The child lay quiet for a few moments, then fell into a deep sleep. She would never cry again.

Brother Irator sat back on his heels. He was seemingly unaffected by the ritual, not a bead of sweat, no signs of breathlessness. The parents listened carefully as the Brother advised them on caring for the infant for the next few days. Although they themselves were sweating and a little agitated, their eyes showed nothing but dull obedience.

After the customary breakfast Irator bid the family farewell, mounted his horse and rode out of the village. He whistled a merry tune as he rode along in the morning sunshine. He was happy with his day's work, another Essence safely captured, another child who would grow up healthy, well fed, in a balanced, orderly society free from poverty, violence and crime. No one taking too much, leaving the weak with leftovers and scraps.

Of course there had to be some such as himself to bear the burden, carrying his Essence within him. But that was a small price to pay for being able to bestow the Gift on others.

Irator turned his horse towards the east and trotted off. Another child to rescue, he thought to himself, and smiled.

Chapter One

From a deep, earthy cave several miles from the nearest village, came a sound not often heard. A girl of about six was rubbing her knee through patched trousers and crying. Large tears ran down her face, matting long dark hair to grubby cheeks.

"Shush dear, you must be quiet, someone will hear." The woman was about forty, but looked much older. She was painfully thin, with a pale, almost yellow complexion. The shapeless dress she wore over patched leggings had seen better days, barely keeping her covered, much less warm.

"But ma, it hurts, I fell over that root over there, why can't I cry when it hurts?" sobbed the girl. The woman coughed against her sleeve, trying to stifle the sound. "I've explained all this before, the Brothers don't like crying, they will take you away from me. You must be brave."

The girl sobbed a few more times, then quieted.

"I don't like the Brothers, and the next one I see I'm going to tell him!"

The woman grabbed at the child and slapped her face, "Kymar, you must never say that again! Promise me you will never say that, if you see a Brother you must hide, do you hear me, hide! run away! never let them near you." She shook the girl's shoulders, "Promise me!"

Kymar sobbed quietly but new tears rolled down her face, leaving slightly cleaner streaks. "I promise ma, I promise." The woman hugged the girl tightly to her, hiding her own tears.

She couldn't stand the thought of her daughter's bright eyes being dulled by the witchcraft of those brutes. For six years she had kept the secret of Kymar's birth. Moving from place to place, caves, tree-houses, holes in the ground. Living hand to mouth and running in the dead of night.

Never enough food, never enough anything. But all this she had gladly suffered to hear her daughter laughing, playing and learning. Kymar was such a bright girl, keen, a fast learner, always eager to know. And always questions, day and night. Sometimes the answers didn't, or couldn't, come. Some things were better not said, not yet.

She coughed again. Being forced to live in this damp hole in the ground wasn't doing her any good. Her coughing was eased by certain herbs, but these weren't always available. The forest provided much of what they needed, but some things were only available in villages. The villages were dangerous places for those with bright eyes.

A rumbling noise startled her out of her reverie. She knew immediately what it was.

"Kymar, come here, sit with mother, and keep very quiet." she whispered.

The girl started to protest, then noticing the look of fear on her mother's face she obeyed. They sat huddled together in the dark cave, waiting for the soldiers to pass.

But this time the soldiers stopped. The girl clung against the woman as a deep voice sounded in the cave entrance. The soldier clumped around for a while then went silent. A few minutes later the unmistakable odour of urine wafted down. There was a loud exchange of banter as the soldier pulled his clothes back on and mounted his horse. The sound of hooves died away. Although the child squirmed impatiently, the woman kept a tight hold until she was satisfied they had really gone. It was time to move on. This was no place for a child.

She vowed that one day her child would walk in the sun, to feel its warmth and marvel at it, to take the time to wonder at its brilliance. Not to see it and not notice, not to feel it and ignore its power, like the others. The dead eyes, the human cattle, slaves to the Warlocks.

Chapter Two

A young boy made his way along a narrow ledge no wider than his foot. His right hand held on to a crumbling stone cliff, his left stuck out in mid-air. He was about sixty feet down from the top of a sheer sandstone cliff, with forty feet below. None of this seemed to bother him. He was twelve years old, of less than average height, with light brown hair, greenish eyes and a wide smile.

The boy's companion followed some twenty feet behind. He wasn't holding on at all, nor was he particularly watching where he was going. He was almost as tall as Garen, wider at the shoulder with longer arms. Although he was only eight, he had matured much faster than his friend, making them equal in most things.

Garen stopped for a moment, steadied himself then turned to watch his friend. Garen was always amazed at the way Sciel could climb almost anything with very little effort. He was a good climber himself, but compared to Sciel he was an old man on crutches.

"Come on Sky, we haven't got all day," grumbled Garen.

"I hungry, can we eat yet?" complained Sciel in a surprisingly deep voice.

"That's all you think about, we can eat after one more go."

With a quick glance at each other the two friends suddenly turned and leapt off the cliff.

Garen slid into the sea with hardly a ripple, long practice had made him good, even for a twelve year old. There was very little else to do, except the chores his father gave him to keep him quiet.

Sciel didn't reach the water. Eight feet short of the calm surface his long, muscled arm shot out, grabbed a slight overhang and brought himself to a dead stop. A human would have been severely injured by this move, but Sciel wasn't human.

"Ah, Sciel! You said you wouldn't do that this time, you promised!" Garen whined from the water.

The ape-like creature hung casually by his three fingers, picking bits of seaweed off the cliff and trying them. After discovering they weren't too bad, and eating a good mouthful, he looked down at Garen. "Don't like getting fur wet, it takes long time to dry. If I don't jump, you don't jump. Don't want to spoil your funny."

"It's fine Sky. I shouldn't make you do it, and it's fun, not funny..."

Garen froze as Sciel's eyes locked on a spot out to sea.

"Boat." He said. A single word that said many things.

Only rarely did the pair see boats of any kind. Mostly they kept far out to sea. No one came to this island by choice. Occasionally they would see boats nearer to shore, the Warlocks travelled to the further villages by boat if the sea was calm. Garen's father had taught him how to spot their kind of craft, Garen had passed the knowledge on to Sciel. They were high sided with a prow at either end. This was such a boat.

Garen kept as low in the water as he could, letting the slight swell move him up and down. He kept his brown hair facing out to sea, hoping that whoever was in the boat would see only a Teff playing with the flotsam. The Teff were of little interest to the Warlocks, but a boy playing, that was a different matter entirely.

Chapter Three

Brother Irator knocked quietly on the sturdy walnut door. A muffled voice that seemed to come from quite a distance away told him to enter. He pushed down the wooden handle and slowly eased the door open. He entered the large room, walked quickly across the carpeted floor and out into a high walled garden. At the far end of the rows of neatly planted fruit bushes a tall figure dressed in a plain brown robe beckoned him. Treading carefully, Irator made his way over.

"No problems at all today, Brother?" Inquired the Head Priest without preamble.

"No, Brother Parsathan, all is well."

Parsathan stooped to set another strawberry plant. He used a silver trowel, which was always spotless, and a steel rule to measure the exact distance between each plant and row.

Parsathan stood to his full six feet and looked down at Brother Irator, fixing him with his brown eyes.

"What of the wild folk living by the coast? They must be located and given the Gift before they hurt themselves."

"Yes, of course Brother Parsathan, but those forests are very dense, there are not enough Peace Keepers to cover the whole area. Krane, even now is setting restraining devices in an effort to enable us to bestow the Gift on these unfortunate few, she hopes to bring you news herself, later today."

A large bee flew past Brother Irator's nose, he froze instantly.

"That is very good, Brother Krane is proving to be a very resourceful woman." A loud buzzing caught their attention. Parsathan turned to the sound, reached into a spider's web and pulled out the bee. He pulled off some of the attached web, then gently let it go. The bee flew around his head twice then disappeared into an old apple tree. "Making her captain of the Peace Keepers was one of my better ideas."

Parsathan pulled another plant from a trug and carried on planting. Irator took this as an end to the conversation, he turned and carefully walked out, keeping both eyes open for bees.

Parsathan was fond of his bees. The last captain had swatted one of them after it stung him on the hand. Parsathan had said nothing, but was seen later in the workshops. That night the captain laid down on his bed, triggering a massive oak hand which had fallen from the ceiling crushing him to death. Parsathan had later claimed the body and added it to his large compost heap.

Chapter Four

Rain fell softly from a grey sky, dripping off the leaves of the tall grey-trunked trees. A fine sea mist rolled slowly across the vale, hiding the young woman from prying eyes.

This is fine weather for grave digging she thought. The ground is soft, the mist hiding the site and muffling the sound. She had been thinking these thoughts for several hours, since discovering the body of her mother in one of those traps. For most people the traps were little threat, a few moments work with a knife and you were out. But mother didn't carry a knife. She lacked the strength to wield one anyway, the disease in her lungs, made worse by this cursed damp, had robbed her of her health. She could barely talk, let alone walk, but she insisted on going to the village for the bi-annual counting, lest she be missed. She had made it there without any problems. Coming back…

Kymar wiped the tears from her eyes, leaving mud streaked across her face. Digging with an old metal dish was bad enough without the added complication of emotion. She could have taken the body, (The body, not my mother, no, not that) into the village and left it for someone to find. But then "They" would have had her again, she would have hated that. So Kymar was determined to bury her near their home of the last three years. Not too near of course, (She could hear her mother saying, so clear, picture her face so sharp) in case "it" was discovered.

The daylight had faded, the sea-mist blown away by the time she had finished. She had left the face uncovered for hours, unable to find the strength to accept the fact that her mother no longer had need of breath. She had cried loudly until a noise in the forest had startled her to awareness. Her mother's long years of training had taken over then, she had quickly filled in the last of the shallow grave, apologising as she did, scattering leaves over it to hide any traces of activity.

Kymar melted silently into the undergrowth, looking back many times in the direction of the unmarked grave, vowing one day to return, to mark the place with the biggest headstone she could carry.

She wandered off through the twilight of the forest, the great grey trunks damp and cold. Her mind wandered too, back to happier times. She realised only too well that happy was a subjective term. The soldiers had rid her of any chance at a normal childhood. But her mother had done her best, setting time aside each day for learning, time for playing, time for sitting and quietly watching the forest. Everything she knew was taught to her by her mother; How to play, how to keep quiet even when you want to cry, how to tell juicy snow berries from poisonous ice berries, how to run away if soldiers neared. How to die quickly when they captured you.

As these thoughts and many years worth of others coursed through her mind Kymar walked, not stopping for rest, food or shelter. Every step was accompanied by a tear. She had a lot of tears, she would wander for a long time.

Chapter Five

Garen was sitting on a fallen log by the side of one of the village fields, his father was digging weeds out from between rows of potatoes. Garen was supposed to be helping but he got bored easily. He was swinging his hoe around like a large sword, pretending to fight the soldiers. His father turned around occasionally, a frown of disapproval on his face.

"Garen, don't do that, someone will notice, then we will both be in trouble."

Garen had long since known of his fathers "condition". His father had managed to explain it to him when he was younger. Apparently different people reacted to the Ripping in different ways. There were some in the village, like his father, who were hardly affected at all, although his father found it very difficult not to do anything a Warlock or soldier asked of him, and he still spent most of his time doing his allotted tasks. But he had managed to keep his only son a secret for almost 17 years. His father had said that Garen had a gift, he had an abundance of Life Energy, so when the Warlocks cast their life-sucking spell over him, they had enough to fill the Death jar, but left Garen with more than enough to carry on with life. His father had noticed this, and for the first four years had kept him calm with a mild drug made from a tree root.

Most were affected quite deeply by the spell, becoming nothing but slaves, workers to grow the food and build the roads for the Warlocks. A few were completely ruined by the Ripping, becoming nothing but mindless idiots. There were no idiots in the villages of course, they seemed to disappear as soon as they were noticed. Then there were those who were completely unaffected, completely free willed. Those that were noticed at a young age, and most were, ended up being recruited into the Brotherhood, where they became Warlocks or were never seen again. A few who managed to evade both Warlock and soldier lived rough in the great forest, the Wild Ones, constantly hunted by the soldiers.

The sound of a jangling harness brought Garen quickly to his feet. He stood behind his father and copied his every motion. A group of six soldiers rode into sight, emerging from the great coastal forest. They looked dirty, very weary and one sported a grey bandage around his leg. They glanced over at the two farmers, but saw very little to interest them.

Once the noise of their passing had gone Garen sat back down. "I wonder what happened to them, they've been fighting, you could tell. But something that fought back ay Dad!" He swung his hoe around his head, threatening to do someone an injury.

His father stopped his work for a moment, "Garen, if you can't help at least go somewhere you won't be seen."

Garen stood the hoe against the log, said "thanks Dad," and ran off into the forest.

He felt a little guilty sometimes. Because of the way his father was he found it very difficult to discipline his son. Garen had been making the most of this for several years. Now he was older and understood more he was starting to be more respectful. Luckily most of his bad behaviour involved disappearing into the forest with his friend Sciel, so not much harm was done.

The Teff was waiting for him in their favourite spot, which happened to be thirty-five feet up in a large funnel tree. The wide branches spreading from a long trunk made an ideal hiding place. The first twenty feet or so of silvery-grey smooth bark was difficult to climb, but after that you could practically walk the rest like stairs.

Sciel greeted him through the usual mouthful of food. He was constantly surprised by how quickly humans became full, after what for him was only a snack. He remembered the amazed look on Garen's face the first time he ate a pig in one sitting. It was only a small pig of course, and he didn't eat all of the bones. They weren't much better with liquids, a few buckets of that ale stuff and they couldn't even walk straight.

The two had been chatting about this and that for sometime when Sciel held a finger to his lips. Garen quieted, looking in the direction of Sciel's gaze.

Through the trees ahead, Garen spotted movement, a furtive shadow against the lighter coloured trees. They both pressed closer to the bough they were sitting on, carefully parting the masses of tiny green leafs. The figure disappeared on the edge of a small clearing some distance ahead. Garen and Sciel glanced at each other then silently stood. They made their way along a branch that led to the next tree, a short hop and they were over. Sciel soon showed his superior agility, slowly building up a good lead over Garen.

Suddenly Sciel stopped and crouched down behind a large clump of leaves. Garen moved slowly behind him and did the same. On the ground across the clearing a hooded figure knelt in the leaf-litter. The figure seemed to be doing something in the earth, but Garen, no matter how far he leaned out, was unable to see what.

The branch Garen was holding began to feel very strange, as though his hand was sliding off it. How could that be when he had a grip better even than a swordsman? Before Garen could react his hand slipped. He snatched at another branch but it was out of reach. His other hand grabbed for Sciel, who wasn't even looking, and found only thin air. Finally he resigned himself to a fall to earth, hoping it wouldn't hurt too much. For some reason he closed his eyes as the patchwork of brown and green leafs approached his head.

A few moments later nothing had happened. He thought either the tree was much taller than he remembered, or someone had caught him. He looked up into the greenery between his legs and saw a long brown furred arm hanging down like some monstrous fruit. Three long fingers and a thick thumb held his ankle in a not too solid, almost casual, grip.

Garen suddenly remembered the business at hand. Upside down he surveyed the clearing, which was rather disappointingly empty.

The arm grew a head and Sciel's face, split by an enormous grin, appeared, "She went that way," he pointed with his chin, "She didn't see you. Want to go up or down?"

Safely back on the ground Garen turned to Sciel, "So, how do you know she's a she, and what do you think she was doing here?"

"She smelt like one of your shes, and she was planting flowers," Sciel pointed with his chin again, both hands being busy shelling a large nut he had found.

Garen carefully crept over to where the mysterious female had been standing, alert for any tricks on her part. The leaf-litter had been disturbed and a tiny forest Bloodflower had been planted.

A sudden chill ran down Garen's back, he quickly stepped away from the spot. Bloodflowers were often planted on graves.

He turned to Sciel who was disappointedly shaking the now empty nut shell, hoping some more would fall out if he did.

"Do you think you could follow her, Sky? Find her again?"

Sciel looked up surprised, "You don't like females, what you want her for?"

"I'm just curious that's all, she's obviously a Freewill like me, my father says there are lots of them out here, fighting for freedom, living their lives the way they want to, not pushed around by those damned Warlocks, I'd join them myself if I could find them... And anyway, when did I say I didn't like fema... girls?"

But the sentence was a little long for Sciel who had lost interest and was sniffing around the forest floor. After a few minutes he stood, looking around. "She doesn't smell much, bit damp really, think I'd know her if I smelled her again." With that he turned towards a tree and practically ran up the trunk.

Garen stood with his hands on his hips shaking his head. He shouted, "Well thanks very much!" Then remembering where he was, added in a quieter voice, "some friend you are."

Sciel pulled a twig from the tree and threw it at Garen, "Only one you got," then ran further up the tree making the strange hissing noise that passed for giggling in the Teff race.

Chapter Six

Kymar was lost, not physically, she knew every inch of this dismal rain damp forest. She had wandered many miles since her mother's passing, (she never thought of it as death, but always as passing, as though she had gone to a distant village and could return any moment) aimlessly meandering among grey trunks.

For many months she had not even cared where she ended the day, dropping down to sleep in a pile of leaves or curled up in the roots of an enormous tree. Lately, over a year later, she had begun to return home at the end of the day, to the dark hollow beneath a large tree she had shared with her mother for so long. The hollow provided her with shelter and what little food she ate when she remembered. But the underground hollow also provided her with memories.

The roots of the forest above ever sought the depths of the earth. Her mother used to cut them back, then make a gluey stew with them, half of which was eaten, the other half used to make cloth waterproof for wrapping food and the few metal items they had.

Kymar hadn't cut them back for a whole year, they were beginning to get in her way. Sometimes she would swat at them angrily when they brushed her face, sometimes she would vent her anger, trying to rip them down. It seemed to her she had enough anger mixed with grief to pull the whole tree down on top of her. But she only ended up hurting her hands. She would then sob quietly (always quietly, Kymar) in the aftermath, clutching her hands to herself, wishing for her mother.

Kymar walked through the forest towards her mother's grave, stopping only to dig up a Bloodflower from its dappled shelter. A full year since her mother's passing, Kymar had decided to stop her grieving but didn't know what to replace it with. So, she would visit the grave today, the first time she had felt able. Then, she said to herself, I will visit once a week, plant small flowers so no one will notice. Afterwards, let fate throw what it will.

The grave site looked undisturbed as she peered cautiously around a large tree. Slowly, one foot after the other Kymar made her way towards the grave. She had approached the clearing from the opposite direction to her hollow, sliding through the forest like the shadow deer; those great grey beasts who moved silently through the undergrowth, melting out of site just by standing still. Her heart pounded in her chest as she neared, the first wetness of tears formed in her eyes. Her breath became irregular, threatening to break up into sobs. The knot in her stomach tightened with every step.

Kymar knew the exact site even though one part of the clearing looked like any other. The day and place of the burial was etched on her mind. Quickly she planted the flowers, said a few words, then hurried away.

Some time later, curled under a worn blanket in the hollow, Kymar examined her emotions. The visit had proved more traumatic then she had thought. She had found it very difficult to stay long. The thought of the body, she shivered, unable to continue the thought. As she had hurried away, the weight of guilt on her shoulders, she thought she heard strange noises and whispering voices. Images of ghosts, from stories told to her by her mother, (was there nothing she did on her own?) ran through her mind making her dash away carelessly.

When she had calmed enough she had returned stealthily home by a circuitous route. Kymar vowed to herself to sort out the long neglected abode, then her long neglected life. Possibly the one would lead to the other.

Chapter Seven

A figure clad in white leather paced up and down outside the walnut door, waiting to be summoned. Krane had heard others say that Parsathan was usually a most understanding man, but wasn't sure whether the people who said this were his spies. She pulled a dagger from her belt and began spinning it around on her finger, a nervous habit that tended to make others nervous.

Finally Brother Irator emerged, leaving the door open.

"You may enter now," he whispered, bowing slightly.

"Thank you Brother," she said sarcastically as he walked past.

Parsathan was sitting behind a large table at one end of the room. Krane was completely unable to gauge his mood from his neutral expression. She walked over to the table, stopping a safe distance away. The Head Priest looked directly at her, saying nothing.

"I am afraid to report that the patient died before we could get any information, sir, he was very weak from malnutrition and had received injuries from the trap and the struggle with the Peace Keepers." She looked straight ahead, sweat beading her forehead.

Parsathan looked out on to his garden sighing, as though that was the only place he found perfection. "Don't worry too much Krane, I'm sure you will find another. At least there is one less Wild One suffering needlessly. You tried the new technique I suggested." It wasn't a question, more an invitation to report the results.

"Of course sir! But by the time we had cut his toes off and fried them in front of him he had died."

"The folk from the villages haven't the same stamina as us from the Fort of Souls, it is hardly surprising they aren't able withstand my cunning persuasions."

"Yes sir, perhaps we will be luckier next time."

The first expression of emotion Krane had seen crossed Parsathan's face, he leaned forward slightly and said in a steady voice, "There is no such thing as luck Brother Krane, you would be wise not to rely on it, good luck is just proper planning, bad luck is pure incompetence." He stressed the last word, looking meaningfully into her eyes.

"Yes sir, of course." She had come to attention at this point, her leather boots cracking together.

Parsathan lifted some papers from an iron box and began to go through them. Krane had been warned about his dislike of hello and goodbye, but was slightly startled seeing it in action. After a few moments she relaxed slightly and left, closing the walnut door quietly behind her.

She walked off down the draughty corridor vowing to do her very best to capture the Wild Ones, to convert them to the Essence, for their own good of course.

Chapter Eight

Garen sat in a large tree, Sciel by his side, watching the soldiers round up some of the villagers for a special work detail. His father was one of the men, he walked along, head hung low like the rest. Garen knew his father resented the soldiers but found it very hard to resist. He suddenly felt guilty about this, then started to get angry, "Why should my father be made to do work he doesn't want to do? Why doesn't somebody do something?"

Sciel put a hand to his brow and began to look around in every direction, finally coming to rest with his gaze on Garen.

"What! What do you expect me to do? I'm only... nearly a man, yes! We could join the Freedom Fighters in the forest, learn to fight then storm the castle."

Sciel looked at Garen and said through a mouth full of leafs, "What you mean, we? I no good at fighting, 'cept you 'course."

Garen ignored the insult, "Well perhaps you could do something else, scout or cook or something. Well, perhaps not cook, there'd be nothing left for the rest of us. But you'd make a good scout, you can climb anything, I sometimes think if I threw a whole Zong fruit into the air you'd climb up to get it."

"No, wait for it to come back down, break open on your silly head and eat it quick."

"Where's you spirit of adventure? Do you want to sit around eating for the rest of your life?"

Sciel grinned hugely.

"Oh forget it, I'll go on my own." mumbled Garen, climbing down the tree. As he suspected Sciel followed slowly behind, trying to get a large caterpillar to walk into his mouth.

They walked for some distance in silence, Garen leading as quietly as he could to where he guessed the Freedom Fighters might make camp. Sciel lagged behind wondering why Garen had to make so much noise.

After several miles the pair had seen no sign of any other humans, never mind Freedom Fighters. Garen was beginning to go off the idea, thinking the rumours he had heard were just stories, made up by the Headmen to pass the time away. The Headmen were like his father, with a little free will of their own. There weren't many of them and none of them knew about Garen, that would have been too risky. They liked to gather together at night and pretend to be free men, at least that's what Garen thought. He would sit just out of range of the firelight, listening to their tales, told with little emotion. Garen's father suspected at least one of them of being a spy.

It began to get dark, so he decided to turn around and head for home. He was just beginning to realise that if there were Freedom Fighters they would live deep in the forest, not near to any place regularly visited by the soldiers. He admitted with a shrug that he would have to go deeper, but not tonight, best go home and prepare properly. Gather some things together; food, spare clothes, a weapon of some kind. Then come back tomorrow and try again.

* * * *

Ten days later Garen was ready, he had managed to garner some smoked fish and dried meat from the evening meal. The clothing he already had, but the weapon had proved elusive. Finally he had settled on a long stick with a bumpy swelling on one end. He demonstrated it to Sciel, "Look, it's a staff to help me walk," He swung it around his head with the swelling outwards, "It's a club, or." Now he stabbed with the other end, "a spear, see?"

"No good against sword, cut in half, then you got two weapon'."

Garen sighed, "Don't be so negative, you obviously

sneak up behind soldiers with a sword and clonk them on the head. Now come on, we've got a long day ahead of us."

"Where my stuff?" grumbled Sciel.

"You don't need stuff, you're covered in fur, you could eat the whole forest given enough time, and you said you didn't like fighting, so come on, let's go."

Garen set off into the forest, Sciel stood where he was picking at the fur on his hands. Garen sighed deeply, pulled out a strip of dried meat and offered it to Sciel, "Here, you can carry this."

Sciel rushed forwards, grabbed the meat, and carried on running, dodging between the trees.

Chapter Nine

Kymar wandered through the mist damp forest, not aimlessly now, but certainly with little purpose. She had taken to walking a different route every day. Sometimes she walked miles, often all day, never stopping, not even to eat. Sometimes, when the sun shone and the birds sang she didn't think of her grief. In the lonelier parts near the coast, away from habitation she saw groups of thin, bedraggled men and women gathered around small fires. She never approached them and they never saw her.

On this particular day she had seen quite a group of them arguing loudly. She couldn't quite make out what they were saying, but she wasn't much interested anyway. Kymar turned and began to walk towards a small thicket, in case any of them turned around. As she stepped between two large trees behind the mass of bushes something brushed her leg. Before she had time to look down a rope snared her ankle, dragging her off her feet. She fell to the wet earth with a thud, then was yanked upwards with a bone wrenching snap. Somewhere above a noise like a firework sounded, and a glowing yellow orb shot into the air. Kymar swung upside down from side to side, twisting with each frantic kick. Her mother had taught her better than to scream, so she used all her fear and anger clawing at the grey bark of the tree beside her.

Several minutes later she realised the futility of the situation, she tried to calm herself down, look at the trap she had blundered into just like her mother. Tears ran down her forehead, through her long hair, which dangled in the mud. Finally when she was almost calm she managed to think clearly. She didn't have much time due to the alarm, the people in the camp would obviously have run at the first sign of trouble, so there was no one to help except herself.

The rope was tightening around her ankle now, her foot had started to go numb. Kymar realised that this wasn't the same type of trap that had killed her mother, the soldiers had improved it by pulling you off your feet instead of just holding you. Her knife was easily reached at her belt, but the rope was a different matter. Kymar tried pulling herself up with her clothes, but no matter how she tried, and cried, she wasn't able to bend that far.

A sudden rustling of leaves made her freeze, she slowly turned around scanning the upside down trees for movement. A pair of brown eyes studied her from the thicket. A few seconds went by, then a large head appeared. A thick grey mane surrounded a face that seemed to be made entirely of teeth. The Wolfbear stalked slowly forwards sniffing at Kymar, suspicious of such an easy meal. Its wide paws made very little sound as it approached, its hot breath smelling strangely sweet as it blew across her face. Kymar refused to close her eyes, she wanted to show her mother how brave she had been when they were re-united.

The Wolfbear patted at Kymar's chest with a clawless foot. This set Kymar swinging and turning dizzily, the white teeth came nearer then disappeared as she spun and twisted around. Her neck muscles spasmed, awaiting the teeth that would soon sink into them.

But the bite never came, one more turn and the beast had disappeared, three more turns and it had been replaced by two sets of stout leather boots. Looking further up, or down, she saw thick leather trousers and drawn swords, soldiers!

"Well well, what have we here? A pretty little Freedom Fighter, and clean as well, whatever next?"

"Still looks a bit skinny though and look at that hair, has it ever been cut?"

Kymar now had something she understood to vent her anger on, her mother had taught her to run at the first sign of soldiers. That was obviously impossible, so the next best thing was to die fighting.

As the rope spun her around again she lashed out with all her strength, driving the small blade still clutched in her hand into the thigh of the nearest soldier. He screamed loudly and toppled backwards dragging the knife out of her grip. The second soldier looked on in dismay, unsure whether to tend to his fallen comrade or kill the girl. Finally the copious amounts of blood and the obvious inability to move on the part of the prisoner made his mind up. He sheathed his sword, pulled a long cloth from a pouch on his belt and tried to stem the flow. With a quick flick he pulled the knife out, making his comrade scream even louder, then tied the bandage tightly around the wound.

When he was satisfied he stood and stormed over to Kymar, whose swing was slowing now. He intended to make this Wild One suffer before he took her back for the Gift. He wasn't sure if he should strip her or punch her. Before he could decide Kymar swung a wide punch at him, catching him in the groin. The steel rivets on the armoured leather dug into both of them, but had a greater effect on the soldier who doubled over, a silent scream on his face.

Kymar had now decided that she didn't want to die, not ever. Not at the hands of these idiot soldiers, not by the magic of the filthy soul stealing Warlocks, not even when the grey carriage arrived at the end of her days, she would fight and scream as the coachman dragged her in.

Kymar had worked out that she could control the swing somewhat by angling her body. She began to swing back and forth as fast as she could until she swung into the soldier standing holding himself. He immediately suspected another attack on his manhood and pulled his knees together. Too late he realised Kymar's plan and could only watch as his sword was pulled from the sheath.

Kymar was surprised by the weight of the sword, but gritted teeth and determination propelled the long weapon towards the rope. The sharp edge bit deep into the rope and for long seconds the only sound was the ripping of the remaining fibres. Then, with a sudden plummet, Kymar's back thudded into the mud floor.

Quickly she rolled over and stood as straight as she could, her ankle hurt like hell, and she couldn't feel her foot. The soldiers had recovered quickly, the one on the ground was sitting upright holding a long dagger. The soldier standing had borrowed his comrade's sword.

She realised she had never held a sword before, much less knew how to use one. She looked at the soldier who seemed to be pointing the blade at her middle, making little circles with the point. Kymar did the same.

"Come on then, boy! Let's see how good you are now I'm upright. We Freedom Fighters have been training for this moment for a long time." Kymar took up what she hoped was a threatening stance, trying to hide the flaming agony clawing up her leg.

A noise sounded somewhere in the trees. The soldier looked nervously around, then began to back off. Helping his wounded partner to his feet, he kept the sword levelled at Kymar.

Slowly, leaving a trail of blood, the two soldiers made a tactical withdrawal, saying only, "Next time…"

Kymar let the sword droop in her hand, standing a while before removing the remains of the noose. To her right a large grey head appeared from behind a bush, its mouth hung open, its eyes locked with Kymar's. "Oh go away you ugly great brute, I've had a long day."

To her everlasting surprise the Wolfbear turned and walked silently away.

Kymar leaned against one of the trees and slumped down it on to the ground. Her ankle was throbbing, pulsing in time to the beating of her heart, loud in her chest. Now that the excitement was over her body seemed to be one long pain. The tendons in her leg felt like they had been stretched, her back ached with a shooting fire, and her neck was beginning to go painfully stiff.

She sat very still for a long time, the bright sword balanced across her canvas leggings. Slowly Kymar lifted first one leg, then the other, causing a reflected sunbeam to run back and forth along the blade. She watched it in fascination for several minutes, going through the events in her mind. Suddenly she stopped, slowly, very slowly, her eyes brightened to match the reflection. Then, a broad smile lit up her face, not a smile of happiness, but a deep, meaningful, dangerous smile.

Chapter Ten

Two dirty, hungry looking figures peered carefully through a dagger bush at a group of very similar people. The larger group were camped under a massive tree with sagging branches, smoke from a pathetic fire drifted up through the large leafs. The three women, seven men and a couple of children talked in whispers, about what Garen couldn't quite hear.

He turned to Sciel who, even though he looked hungry had actually eaten, was still eating, a large bird he had captured that morning. Leaning closer to Sciel he whispered, "What do you think? Should we go in?"

"Don't know," said Sciel in his normal voice, "p'raps got some food."

The quiet whispers immediately stopped, several of the people drew weapons, walking cautiously towards the bush.

Garen was convinced this was the best time to step forwards, before they started searching the place with long knifes. The group froze as soon as he revealed himself. Those at the back seemed to have melted away, taking the children with them.

"Hello, my name is Garen, this is my friend Sciel, we've come to join you."

Some of the group stood motionless before the pair whilst others carried on around the back of the dagger bush. After a few moments of rustling, hacking and chopping, they reappeared shaking their heads.

A short, very thin man dressed in mud coloured clothes looked them up and down with small dark eyes. His dark hair hung matted down to his shoulders, small twigs and bits of leaf hung among the strands. His skin was muddy brown, not obviously dirty, more a dark tan. He spoke in a quiet, rather hoarse whisper, "What do you want?

Who sent you? You're not spies are you? What you doing running round with a dog rat?"

Garen concentrated for a minute, then replied, "We want to join the battle for freedom, nobody, no, we are not, he's not a dog rat, he's a Teff and he's my friend."

The man had lost interest in both his questions and the answers Garen had given, except for the one about the battle.

He looked at the others then looked towards the sky, making a strange hissing noise that Garen was relieved to discover was laughter.

"Freedom Fighters," he stepped in close to Garen, his breath almost stunning him backwards, "Freedom Fighters is who you're looking for? Well I've got news for you young scrag, there's precious little of either of those around here, freedom's a flexible thing, hear? And in these conditions there isn't a lot of fight to go around either. So go back to which ever Warlock sent you and give him this." The man swiftly lifted his knee, connecting firmly with Garen's recently developed manhood. Garen stood fixed in place, his hands clamped across the pain, his teeth clamped together. He had never felt such pain, such shock, physically and mentally, that one man could do that to another was previously unthought of.

The small group re-assembled and wandered away grinning, at least one of them keeping an eye on them until they were out of sight. Garen suspected that one or two of them would hang back to ensure they didn't follow, but he was physically unable to walk properly, never mind conquer the mental block involved.

Sciel looked at him with a strange expression on his face, Garen realised he was suppressing a smile.

"Keep ours on inside, much safer." Sciel's smile finally burst through, he stepped quickly out of range.

When Garen had recovered enough he paced up and down, looking around. "Well, what are we going to do now? We came all this way for nothing, three days with not a thing to eat but dried meat and berries. Well, there is only one thing to do, do it ourselves. Storm the fort, break the jars and release all the captured souls." Garen stood proudly as though the deed was almost done. "Come on, we've got work to do."

Garen strode purposefully, though slightly bow-legged, away into the trees. Sciel stood for a moment, waited until his human friend had returned and set off in the proper direction then followed behind.

* * * *

In the afternoon of the second day, as Sciel was explaining to Garen how babies were made, the pair walked right into an ambush. Garen had been laughing in disbelief when two armed men suddenly appeared in front of them. Footsteps behind told them another had cut off their escape. Garen immediately assumed the dead-eyed look and submissive stance his father had taught him, but it was too late, the soldiers had heard him laughing, that was always a give away.

The soldiers advanced slowly, seemingly wary, until the sword points swayed an arms length away.

"On your knees." The one in charge said firmly.

Garen stayed standing, then realised too late that had been a test, no slave would have been able to disobey. The soldier smiled, a thin smile on a thin face, staying on his guard. "So, a Wild One! You don't look bad on it though, someone been looking after you have they?" When Garen didn't answer he leared, "The Brothers will soon get it out of you, don't you worry about that." His blue eyes twinkled, one side of his face screwing up as he tried to wink.

Garen's thoughts turned to his father, he had to escape, get away from here, he couldn't let them make him talk even if it meant… He was unable to finish the thought. Instead he looked the soldier straight in the eye, something else the slaves found impossible.

To his dismay he realised how badly prepared he was, the soldier was dressed in thick leather, top to toe. In places the leather was reinforced with small circular metal plates. He wore thick gauntlets with spiked metal strips across the knuckles, and similar boots. He carried a sword as long as Garen's arm, a dagger and a club in his belt. On his head sat a round leather hat with a metal brim, the edge of which seemed to be sharpened. The other soldier, who seemed very young to be in this line of work, wore the same, but with a long bow and quiver across his back.

Garen had even lost the staff he carried, it had stuck in the mud of a stream they had forded, he couldn't be bothered to retrieve it at the time. But as Sciel had said, not much good against swords. They had also been walking on the forest floor, up in the trees they would have been safe, but Garen had been over-confident. He hadn't expected there to be soldiers this far into the woods, certainly not on foot.

Garen was about to speak when he heard a sound behind him, a blinding flash ripped across his mind and all went black.

He came around a minute later, lying against the furry leg of Sciel. Garen was glad his friend had stuck around, even though he was sure he could easily have got away. A hazy face formed in front of him. The soldier from the back judging by the unfamiliar features. He had a hawk nose, receding chin and a very wide mouth. "That's just a warning, you give trouble, you get double back, double trouble like," he laughed, "Hey, that's good, double trouble, it rhymes, hear!" He stood proudly.

The other soldiers looked knowingly at each other, then shook their heads.

Garen was yanked to his feet by the still laughing soldier. "Your dog rat trained is he?" asked the soldier placidly.

Garen glared at the man, but said nothing. Sciel silently marked him down for breakfast. The two soldiers from the front turned and walked away, the one behind indicated they should follow by jabbing a long curved knife into Garen's back. Then he took up position a few paces behind.

After two or three hours of fast walking in this formation the soldier in charge suddenly stopped and held up a hand. The other two halted forcing Garen and Sciel to do the same. The two in front crept slowly forward between two massive trees that flanked the path. Just before they reached the trees they halted, listening, looking from side to side, then carried on forward. As the first man stepped between the trees he was suddenly dragged off his feet and into the air, dropping his sword, screaming loudly for assistance. The second soldier, the young looking one, dashed forward to help.

From behind Garen came a strange cut off yell that ended in a gurgle. Garen turned slowly around, to see the front of the man's armour bulge then deflate like a pair of bellows. Blood began to run out from the waistline, trickling around the metal plates and down to the floor. Garen was so fascinated he almost forgot where he was. Finally the soldier dropped to the floor. Garen staggered back, yelling out loud. A young girl stood behind, long hair flowing in the breeze, fire burning in her eyes, teeth clamped together in a grin of death. She held the sword effortlessly in one hand, the bloodied tip swaying in a figure of eight pattern.

A witch, Garen thought, we're all going to die. The girl pushed passed a stunned Garen, under the rapidly climbing backside of Sciel, towards the other soldiers. Before he could stop himself Garen called, "Lookout!"

The young soldier turned his head, his eyes widened in amazement. He hesitated, not wanting to drop a superior, who he had been holding up, but fearfully aware of the approaching blade.

In the end his self-preservation won, he dropped the soldier and reached for his own sword. The soldier in command hung motionless puzzled by these new events, trying to work out what was happening from a different perspective. The girl thrust the sword towards the young soldier who staggered back at the right moment, his own sword held uselessly out of the way. The sword carried on forward, seeming to slide effortlessly into the neck of the trapped man. He didn't make a sound, just went glassy eyed as the blood almost fell in one piece from his body.

The young soldier turned away and vomited into a bush, Garen was doing the same not far behind. The girl turned her attention to the young soldier, not worried that his back was turned.

"No!" croaked Garen, "Not like that, you've won, can't you see? It's over."

The girl looked around, as though these acts had been done by someone else. The fire left her eyes, she physically slumped, the sword suddenly becoming too heavy. The girl looked at the soldier cowering behind a sapling, then at Garen. She walked over to Garen dragging the tip of the sword through the damp earth. She stopped in front of him, studied his face for a moment, then thumped him as hard as she could, sending him sprawling flat on his back. "You warned them, I thought they had caught you, but you're one of them!" She spat the last word.

Garen started to scramble to his feet then thought better of it, he didn't know much about girls but if they were all like this one he didn't want to know. "No, no I'm not, they captured me and Sciel, my friend up there," he pointed upwards, the girl didn't look.

"We were in the forest looking for the Freedom Fighters, but we couldn't find them." Garen frowned as Sciel giggled from his high branch. "But you must be with them, to fight like that, and you've got a sword." He said the last word almost with awe.

The girl wasn't yet satisfied, "Why did you warn them?"

"I... I didn't I was warning Sciel, my friend, up there."

He pointed again, this time she looked up, briefly.

"What is it?, It looks like a dog rat."

Garen jumped to his feet, speaking in a firm voice, "He's not an it, he's a Teff, and he's my friend. His name is Sciel, mine is Garen," he looked at her questioningly.

The girl ignored the look, "So, you want to be a Freedom Fighter? What exactly would you do?"

"I already am a Freedom Fighter and I've got everything worked out, storm the fort, break the jars and release the prisoners."

"Yes that's very good, storm the fort on your own. How do you know what will happen when you break the jars? I suppose you know exactly where the prisoners are as well?"

"And I suppose you have a better plan do you? I suppose you know exactly what to do Mrs clever... what is your name anyway?"

"My name is Kymar, not that it's any of your business, I don't need a plan because I'm not a Freedom Fighter, and anyway I've killed more soldiers than you." She hefted the sword over one shoulder then walked away.

Garen called after her, "There's more to it than killing you know!" He looked up at Sciel who had found a birds egg, "Let's follow her, she'll only get into trouble carrying that big sword."

Sciel sighed softly, dropped to the ground cracking the egg on the way, then followed Garen, sucking noisily on the yolk.

The over-looked young soldier stared wide-eyed after the two strangers as they casually trailed off into the forest, a monkey-thing following a few paces behind. Then, coming to his meagre senses, he quietly sneaked away unnoticed.

Chapter Eleven

Kymar was confused, she wandered through the forest towards home seemingly unaware. Her thoughts were racing, going over the events time and time again. What had happened? Where had the strength come from? Now, with it all over she felt sickened by what she had done, but then, before...

She was wandering as usual, she had taken to carrying the sword since the incident with the soldiers. Then out of nowhere more soldiers had appeared, apparently leading a captive boy and a strange hairy creature. She had been just behind them when they emerged from a thicket, none of them had noticed her so she decided to follow. Then the fool in the lead had blundered into one of the soldier's own traps. This is where things went strange. She remembered a sudden impulse springing into her head, a chance for revenge, to pay them back for her mother's death. The sword had suddenly jumped to life in her hand, it was lighter, somehow easier to wield.

The walk towards the soldier bringing up the rear had seemed very short, he was suddenly there in front of her, his back to her, totally unaware. The sword slid in very easily, Kymar shivered in revulsion at the memory. The soldier dropped to the floor, she remembered vague shapes, one of which had scrambled up an over hanging branch. The boy shouted a warning, she couldn't remember what, then the sword had plunged forward again, towards the second man. She had missed, she knew that, but by a quirk of fate the sword had simply carried on under it's own weight, piercing the neck of the one in the trap. The crimson image of the soldier's blood filled her mind, she was appalled that she could do such a thing. She had turned on the young soldier, not seeing a face but a uniform.

Was it possible she could hate something so much that hate just took over? She realised her teeth were still clenched tightly together. She tried to relax, opening her mouth and breathing deeply.

Now it seemed she had picked up a following, the boy and the monkey, the Teff, were following right behind. Well, she needed some company after so long alone. Perhaps they would prove useful.

* * * *

Garen and Kymar were sat around a small fire on thick logs. Sciel was in his usual place in the tree above Kymar's home in the ground. He was eating some kind of snake with fins he had caught in the stream. Kymar was amazed he could fit so much into such a small space. Garen said he digested his food straight away, so that the first mouthful had gone before the last was even swallowed. Sciel added little to the conversation, mainly correcting Garen's exaggerations, but he was supposed to be on lookout anyway.

They had both told each other everything they knew about the Warlocks, the fort and the soldiers. It seemed they both knew a lot of stories, but much of it made sense. Some of the stories contradicted each other, but others seemed to fit together.

Kymar was amazed how little she knew about the outside world, even though her mother had taught her everything she knew, even the messy things men and women sometimes did to make babies. But it was mostly theory, she was sadly lacking in experience. She had come to like Garen in the week they had been here. He was a bit immature, sometimes moody, but mostly he seemed to care what happened to people, specially his father whom he missed a lot. The friendship with Sciel appeared strange at first, but after getting to know Sciel better they seemed almost made for each other. Kymar wished she had a friend like that sometimes.

Garen was quite relieved to find Kymar wasn't a witch, she had laughed loudly when he had told her, her long hair shimmering down her back, she wasn't even half as violent as her dramatic appearance seemed to suggest. He was very surprised to find that had been her first attack with the sword. He had found the story about the way she had come across the weapon very amusing, partly because he didn't believe it, not all of it anyway. Garen had practised a few swings with it himself and found it extremely heavy. He decided to find a lighter weapon. Garen was surprised at the depth of knowledge Kymar had, when it came to living in the forest she was almost as good as Sciel.

"So, we are agreed," said Garen

"Well, it all seems to fit," Kymar replied, "The Warlocks have somehow found or invented a magic spell that takes part of the soul out of the body. They put the soul into a magic jar and seal the top. Then they take the jar and put it in a massive room inside the fort with thousands of others. If the jar gets broken the soul flies out of a window searching for the other half until it re-enters the body. Then that person is back to normal, no longer a slave."

"That's right, but people are different, some are weak willed, so they are destroyed by the ripping, some are stronger and become slaves of various kinds. Some are stronger still like my father, so he cannot disobey the soldiers, but he has kept me secret for many years. Then there are still others who are strong enough to run away but that's all." Garen paused, looked at Kymar and smiled. "Just occasionally, once every however often a child is born with a very strong essence, so strong that the Warlocks have enough to fill the jar but more than enough remains so that the child remains completely free-willed. And that is us". Garen sat back proudly, a huge grin across his face.

"But that still leaves many questions unanswered," added Kymar. Garen's face lost its grin. "Like; if the Warlocks have magic spells to capture souls, what other magic do they have? And if they do have other magic why don't they use it on us? What happens to the jars when someone dies?"

"Where do the soldiers come from?"

"How do we get into the fort, and most importantly, where are the jars kept?"

They looked at each other for a while, silently appraising each other, together but not yet a team. Kymar broke the silence.

"From what I've seen the soldiers are pretty slack, I don't think they expect much trouble. We could just walk into the fort and have a look around."

"I suppose it's worth a try, but not dressed like this, they'd spot us straight away, slack or not."

She thought for a while, then said, "What about the uniforms of the soldiers I...attacked? We could patch them up and use those, just march in as though we own the place."

Garen pulled a face, "Yeuch, I bet they're all covered in blood now, we'd have to scrub them first, if they're still there. That young soldier will have raised the alarm, that wood is crawling with troops now."

"This forest is a pretty big place," said Kymar, "That soldier was pretty shook up. He wouldn't know one funnel tree from another. I'll bet he's wandering the forest even now. Surely it's worth having a look, we can get you a sword as well."

Garen had learned already that Kymar was a very stubborn young lady, if she had made her mind up, not much changed it. But he had learned how to dilute her impulsiveness.

"So, alright, we can go and have a look, Sciel can scout the place out, if everything looks safe and the uniforms are still there we'll give it a try."

Sciel dropped a half-eaten thunder-bug on Garen's head, the inedible end of course, "If man-soldier still there, no need scout, we smell from here," He clamped two fingers over his wide nose, "Pooooo!"

Garen and Kymar laughed, rather nervously, then quickly changed the subject. Kymar picked up a small stick and began poking it into the fire until it was alight. "How do we stand now do you think? We can obviously stay in the forest, but are we safe here? If that soldier did raise the alarm we may be better off moving, deeper in, or towards the coast?"

Garen, trying to answer all her questions in the right order thought for a few moments, watching her wave the lighted twig in front of her face. It made her deep hazel eyes shine like fresh rain on acorns. He had been having thoughts like this for some time. Since meeting Kymar anyway. He looked away quickly, in case she turned and caught him looking. "I think we are alright at the moment, we can stay here as long as we like, there's plenty of food, water and shelter. Have you ever been bothered by the soldiers here?"

Kymar looked up startled, dropping the twig, "Soldiers? Here? No, of course not! They never come here, that's why we... I live here."

Garen was taken aback by her sudden panic. He was mystified by her reaction, not knowing what else to do he answered her last question. "I have seen the Freedom Fighters living by the coast, they seem a ragged bunch, perhaps we would be better off moving further in, to the heart of the forest."

Kymar sat quietly for several minutes, Garen thought it best to follow suit. Eventually she spoke in the quietly confident voice he was used to hearing, "That would take us further from the fort, that's not really what we want is it?"

"No, it would be too far to plan a proper assault, but we could set up a temporary base there, as a sort of bolt-hole if something goes wrong. Then use this place to launch our attack from."

"Yes, good idea, but first we get some sleep, then see about those uniforms, first light so be ready." Kymar turned away and crouched down in a hollow in the ground, a quick shuffle forwards and she disappeared into her home in the ground. Garen followed a little later, crawling on all fours until he reached the crumbling mud stairs that ran down into the hole.

It was very cramped inside, damp and smelled of oil from years of lamps and candles. A thick curtain had been set up across half of the room, Garen could hear Kymar moving around on her side. She had managed to get the one bed, the chest and the chair in there, Garen had to make do with a wonky stool and a folding cot that refused to sit on all four legs all the time. He also had the doorway on his side, which was blocked off with an old table top and a rock at night. Sciel refused to enter the hole, saying the tree would fall into it while he slept, so instead he made a nest in the branches above.

Garen didn't much like it down here, he could hear the clicking, crawling noises made by things in the earth, and the fine roots hanging from every surface made him think he was in the nose of some grotesque creature. The roots came alive at night, tiny bugs and creeping things wandered around hunting and eating on the roots, dangling off the ends or flying from one to another. He closed his eyes, pulled the rough blanket over his head and tried to sleep.

Chapter Twelve

Parsathan walked slowly up and down between a row of low fruit bushes. Three paces behind him Irator tried to keep up with the Head Priest's long stride, but without getting too close. Parsathan snapped his pruning shears at stray shoots, a sure sign that he was angry. Just inside the door of Parsathan's office Krane stood nervously to attention, she couldn't quite hear the conversation, even in the quiet of the priest's garden.

"I am sorry to say Brother that we have had another little incident." Irator was saying.

"How little was this incident Brother Irator, smaller than the last 'little incident'? How many Peace Keepers have come home without their swords this time?"

"I am afraid it was bigger Brother, it appears that two Peacekeepers have been lost."

Parsathan turned to look at Irator, "When you say lost Brother Irator of course you mean not found, as in wandering the forest somewhere, attacked by…what was the word they used?…ah yes hordes…of Wild Ones?"

"I am sorry to say that no, that is not the case. I mean lost as in murdered Brother."

Parsathan swatted angrily at a passing wasp, missing and nearly taking Irator's eye out with the shears, "Brother Irator, give me the plain facts as they happened, don't embellish them with niceties. I am not a man to waste words."

Irator took a breath and carried on, "I'll do my best Brother but you must understand that no witnesses remain to give a true and proper…"

"Brother Irator," interrupted Parsathan, "Please, the facts, I don't have all day, there is a nasty case of seeping throddle in the vegetable patch that must be attended to."

"Yes Brother Parsathan, forgive me. Now, it seems that one of our patrols came across a rather gruesome scene in the forest, near the village of Cliffsedge. Tenner Barta Foxberry was found hanging dead from a tree by his ankle, Private Lunsa was found a short distance away also dead, both having been stabbed by a large weapon, possibly a sword. Private A-te was nowhere to be found and has not yet returned, he is presumed dead. The manner of Tenner Foxberry's death is fairly strange, it seems he was cut in the neck and his blood was drained away."

Parsathan suddenly stopped clipping and turned to Irator. "You mean like in some kind of ritual? A rite of magic?"

Irator was taken aback by this unusual show of emotion, "I-I It's-not really possible to say for certain, but surely the magic has all gone? All but the spells in our keeping."

Parsathan regained his composure, "Yes of course you are right. This is just the Wild Ones getting out of control. I said this would happen if they weren't dealt with. Now, go and tell Brother Krane not to worry herself, I am sure she is doing a fine job of tracking down these murderers."

"Yes Brother, even as we speak two tenners of Peace Keepers are setting up an ambush where the attack took place, using Tenner Foxberry's sword and armour as bait. I believe they have made some rather clever dummies."

Parsathan smiled, turned and walked slowly away down the row of bushes, Irator took his cue and headed back inside.

"Well Brother, what is it to be?"

"He said not to worry Captain Krane, he has every confidence in you, he says you are doing a wonderful job!"

Krane turned away, biting her lower lip. She was even more worried now. Irator walked briskly off to his room to attend to his duties, a broad, saintly smile clamped firmly across his face.

Chapter Thirteen

Garen, Kymar and Sciel had crawled stealthily along the branches of funnel trees for several hundred paces. Now, just ahead they could make out the two bodies of the soldiers Kymar had killed four days ago. Sciel wrinkled his nose at the smell of blood wafting towards them. Kymar gave the agreed signal and they withdrew to a safe distance.

"Well, what do you think? It all looks quiet, the swords are certainly still there," said Garen brightly.

"It's likely that they haven't found them yet, but I'll bet they are still looking. We need that stuff if we are going to get anywhere, but it's not worth taking needless risks. One of us should go, the others stay behind in case something goes wrong."

Garen smiled, "You are very practical aren't you? I wouldn't have thought of that."

"It's just common sense, come on. I'll approach along the ground you follow in the trees. Then I'll grab the stuff and meet you back here."

Garen was too thrown by the common sense remark to argue, before he knew it Kymar was moving towards the intended target. She moved like a shadow, like her mother had taught her, among the trees, keeping low, using every piece of cover. Garen and Sciel followed just behind and above, easily keeping pace along their aerial walkway.

A drop of water landed on Kymar's cheek as she crept forward. She looked through a gap in the canopy to see a grey sky filled with rain clouds. It didn't bother her too much, it certainly didn't put her off the task in hand. She had lived in damp places most of her life so a bit of rain was not a problem.

The gang of three crept closer to their target, slowing to a crawl as they neared the bodies. They were closer now than when they had spied out the place earlier, Kymar was almost close enough to touch one of the swords, which was stuck in the ground behind the next tree.

The entire forest seemed to stand still as Kymar leaned around the tree and reached for the sword hilt. Her hand moved steadily forward, another half step and she would have it.

Up above Garen watched with baited breath, The blood pumping through his body sounded loud in his ears, drowning out every other sound. Even Sciel had stopped looking for food and crouched wide-eyed at Garen's side.

Kymar's finger tips walked slowly across the leather grip of the sword, curling around the handle. She leaned a little further forward, her thumb and finger tips were getting closer now, almost touching. She could feel the cool clammy leather against the palm of her hand.

A voice suddenly rang out shattering the illusion of stillness. "Oh come on let's go home, I'm sick of lying here, and now it's raining on top of everything else."

Kymar pulled back and flattened herself against the tree. She had a fleeting glimpse of a figure swathed in grass and twigs rolling onto his front and getting up.

Another voice spoke, "Yeah, might as well, nobody in their right mind is going to come back to this place, not in this weather anyway. You better wake the others up, Krane'll just 'ave to think of something else."

There was a general noise of people stirring in the under growth, as several heavily camouflaged figures revealed themselves. Kymar realised with a start that she was exposed to some of them. She looked around for a bolt-hole, but there was no cover she could get to quickly without making a noise. Something touched her on the shoulder, only her instincts stopped her from crying out. Looking up she saw a long hairy arm had descended from the branch above her. Eagerly she grabbed it and was hoisted straight up with incredible speed. Sciel sat on a branch grinning at her with his several rows of teeth. Kymar smiled back briefly then turned to study the scene below.

Across the way in his own hiding place Garen had watched with horror as the forest seemed to come alive with soldiers. Everywhere he looked a tussock of grass or a fallen log had turned into a man, like the forest had given birth to dark creatures from its own leafy floor. He had sat panic stricken when he realised his new friend was clearly visible should the soldiers choose to look in her direction. Sciel had not been so startled, he had simply leapt, almost from a sitting position, across the gap, landing without a sound.

After what seemed like hours, during which Garen was sure he hadn't taken a breath, the soldiers finally walked away, taking the swords and armour with them. They had pulled the grass and twigs from various parts of their clothing, now they were complaining loudly about insects and mud in their underwear.

When all was quiet again and the soft noises of the forest had returned the three met up on the forest floor.

"I was so close, did you see that, I almost had it, we're going to have to think of something else." Kymar sounded annoyed.

"But they nearly caught you, if it hadn't been for Sciel they probably would have. How can you be so calm? Do you know what they would have done to you if they had caught you?"

Kymar shrugged, "They would have taken me to the castle, which is where we want to go isn't it?" She turned and walked away.

Garen stood with his mouth open for a moment, trying to think of something smart to say. The only thing that came out was "Yes, but…"

They all tramped back to Kymar's home under the tree. As usual Sciel refused to enter, instead climbing the tree to his favourite branch. Inside Kymar and Garen sat around a small wooden table on sawn logs, drinking a greenish herbal tea from wooden bowls.

"So what's the plan now?" asked Garen between sips.

"The best thing to do now is go to the castle, have a look around, see if it gives us any ideas. We don't have to actually go in, but if an opportunity happens while we are there we should be ready." Kymar drank deeply from her steaming bowl.

"Are you sure that's such a good idea? We don't have any disguises or weapons. What will we say if we are spotted?"

Kymar filled her bowl up again from the small iron pan on the fire. "We don't need to say anything, people must go in and out of the castle every day. We can just act dumb if anyone approaches, like this..." Kymar let her mouth sag open, hung her head and went glassy-eyed, in imitation of the slave workers.

Garen laughed, "Stop it, you'll stay like it if the wind changes."

So they agreed to visit the castle, just to have a look.

The rest of the night was spent talking of other things; Garen's father, Kymar's mother, Sciel, childhood memories, until they both drifted off to sleep under the creeping roots.

* * * *

The dawn saw them already on their way west towards the castle of the Warlocks. They were ill prepared, Garen carrying a stout staff, Kymar her sword, now wrapped in a length of brown cloth. Both had sacks, containing a few spare clothes and what meagre personal items they had, tied to their backs. Neither had much idea of what to do nor any experience of dealing with soldiers or Warlocks on a daily basis. But they both had pockets full of enthusiasm, and the optimism of youth, which kept them smiling on the long walk.

Sciel merely followed behind, feeling a little left out now his friend had someone else to play with. He had no possessions of his own, he had thick fur and hard feet, had no intention of fighting soldiers and so didn't really need anything. How can anybody move freely with all that lot he said to himself, several times.

The first night was spent in a barn on the edge of the coastal forest. Although they had yet to come across any soldiers, they waited until dark to creep into the barn. None of its doors were locked of course, there was no need for that, another advantage given to them by the Warlocks. The barn had proved to be a good choice to spend any time in. It was warm and dry, had plenty of straw for bedding and proved to be a storage place for fruits of all kinds. Sciel hungrily set about the fruit bins until his face was red and yellow with sticky juice. Garen and Kymar ate a more leisurely supper.

They settled down to sleep in a pile of straw behind a wall of tall barrels. After walking most of the day, with only a short stop for a bite to eat, all three were soon asleep. Neither Garen nor Kymar had given any thought to setting a watch, so they were all still asleep when the farm workers arrived.

Orange sunbeams cast long shadows across the barn entrance. Several burly farmhands had thrown the doors open and had begun rolling empty barrels onto a long cart. Garen was startled awake by the clamping of a hand across his mouth. Looking up through sleepy eyes he saw Sciel, one finger over his lips. He took the hint, rolling slowly over then lifting up to peer through a gap between the barrels. Kymar was standing up with her back against the wooden barricade watching the farmhands closely.

With the cart full it trundled away, the workers following behind. Kymar walked over to the door to check they had all left.

"They've all gone, let's get going." Kymar began to pick up her stuff.

"That was close," sighed Garen, "We had better make sure someone stays awake tonight, they could have lead the soldiers to us. Besides, shouldn't we have left earlier?" He looked to Kymar for an answer.

"These people are no threat, but it might be a good idea to arrive and leave at twilight. We'll have to take it in turns to watch. Come on, it's too late for that now, we will just have to bluff it out if we're stopped." Kymar walked off like someone who had been doing this for years.

"Long as took empty boxes, not bothered." said Sciel through a mouthful of pink Rorabo fruits.

That day and the two after went smoother, they neatly avoided a couple of mounted patrols and a village search party, found an empty cottage to spend the night, and feasted on borrowed fruits from the barn.

It was late morning on the fourth day when they reached the farmlands at the western end of a chain of mountains. On a plateau a good way up the foothills, overlooking the surrounding countryside and the waters of Huclan bay, stood a round castle. Its sand coloured walls and the greenery around it made it look very inviting, not at all what they had expected. Garen would almost have looked for another, one darker and more sinister, if it wasn't for the fact that this was the only castle on the whole island.

The trio stood looking up at it for several minutes, then, the silence broken by Sciel sucking on a gulls egg, Kymar spoke "Come on, there's work to be done."

They set off through the quiet fields, passing the usual slow witted farmhands as they went. It seemed to Garen that Kymar grew quieter, more brooding with each group they encountered.

As the sun started to set, casting long mountain shadows across the pastures, they came across a steep road cut straight through the gently rising hills. It was well tended, very broad and showed signs of the passing of many horses. It seemed to lead right to the castle.

Kymar and Garen looked at one another, silently agreeing to keep off the road, at least until morning. They quickly found a small barn and settled down for the night.

* * * *

Early next morning they were awoken by shouting, and the lumbering creak of a large wagon. Peering through a gap in the wall they could just make out the long wagon, being pulled by six oxen. Slouched in the seat of the wagon was a thin man who managed to produce an ear-shattering noise, which seemed to keep the oxen moving.

Several minutes later a herd of cows were driven past by an old man and three black dogs. The road got busier as the sun rose, with people, carts and various livestock going in both directions.

Kymar suddenly stood up and rushed out, "Come on!" she shouted over her shoulder, "We can mix in with the crowds".

Before Garen could say what about Sciel she was gone, he had to rush to catch up with her, Sciel bounding along behind.

"Slow down Kymar, there's no rush, and what about Sciel?"

Kymar suddenly looked horrified, how could she be so dumb? What if these people haven't seen a Teff before?

The people they past or walked beside studied Sciel quite closely, but none of them said anything or seemed shocked or concerned. They probably aren't capable of that much reaction thought Garen sadly. As the day wore on he noticed many of the people stop by the roadside to eat. There didn't seem to be any joy in their meal, men, women and children all simply sat down and ate whatever they had in a mechanical fashion. Remembering the encounter with the soldiers, Garen tried not to smile. On the occasions when he did the smile was never returned.

The road proved to be longer than it looked, taking them most of the day to reach the bottom of the plateau on which the castle stood. The road steepened sharply, then after a few miles began to zigzag across a wide hill on it's way to the top.

As they rounded the last bend a commotion started somewhere down the hill. Looking back they could see soldiers making their way through the herds, pushing people and cattle aside as though there was no difference. Kymar looked to Garen then assumed the slack-mouthed pose she had demonstrated before. Garen was only just able to control his smile as the soldiers rode by. Sciel tried to hide behind Garen but the soldiers didn't seem interested.

About two hundred paces from the gate the trio halted. Guarding the gate and checking everyone that entered, stood at least a handful of soldiers.

"What do we do now?" whispered Garen, trying to look inconspicuous.

"We just walk in of course, say we have business inside."

"What business? How do we know what goes on in there?"

"Well, it must be market day judging by this lot, we'll say we've come to buy a pig."

A large cart loaded with animal pelts rolled slowly towards them. The driver looked towards them, a very slight smile on his face. Garen looked towards the man, then at the load. "Quick, hide in there under those pelts."

Garen ran towards the cart and clambered over the side. He quickly buried himself in pelts. Kymar walked round to the back of the cart, sat on the low tailgate, then brought her feet up. She was unable to fully cover her face, it reminded her too much of being buried, so she wrapped a large cow hide around herself, forming a deep hood she could see out of. Sciel leapt into the moving cart after Garen, landing with a dull 'ouch' on Garen's head. Sciel burrowed noisily but mostly ineffectively into the skins until only his rear end stuck out. Despite the smell from the cured hides they managed to stay hidden, and luckily Sciel's fur was a similar colour and texture to some of the others. The driver had looked at their antics once then looked away uninterested. The cart trundled steadily towards the gate.

A few minutes later they felt the cart rock to a halt. Voices sounded, seemingly right next to Garen.

"What is your business here?" Said a gruff male voice.

The driver replied, very softly "I have been sent to sell these pelts to the clothes makers."

After a brief look into the back of the cart the soldier yelled self-importantly, "Move on, be quick about it."

The cart jerked into motion again. Another voice, this time female, spoke "What a stink, what have you got in there?"

The man replied in the same placid voice without stopping, "Mixed horse and cow hides, some pig skins, my dinner, a bottle of water, two young people and a Teff."

Garen groaned inwardly, sure enough several voices yelled at once.

"Stop, what did you say?"

"Search the wagon, pull those skins off,"

"Watch out they might be dangerous."

The sound of many swords being pulled from their scabbards joined the general clamour. A cold rush of air and sudden daylight revealed Garen to the soldiers. Kymar was soon found too. She leapt to her feet, unwrapping the sword and yelling death threats at whoever would listen. But skins tangled around her feet and hampered her movement, she was unable to parry the blow that thudded into her leg. She fell forwards screaming, out of the cart and head first onto the cobbles.

Garen didn't know what to do, Sciel had disappeared over the side and underneath the cart, the soldiers were even now poking at him with short spears. The guards on Garen's side grabbed him, dragging him out by his arms. The last thing he saw before a leather hood was crammed over his head was Sciel racing along the backs of the startled oxen, leaping off the lead's head and losing himself in the market crowds.

Cursing his inability to fight he belatedly began to kick and struggle, he had managed to tear one arm free when a blow knocked him off his feet. All sound around him ceased, the darkness under the hood was transformed into a swirl of colour, he felt the hard cobbles under his back, then nothing more.

Chapter Fourteen

Someone was talking to her, she knew that, but the throbbing pain in her head wouldn't let her understand. Kymar tried to touch her head, to feel the damage done by the fall, but her arms weren't moving. So, resigned to her fate she relaxed back into a troubled sleep.

* * * *

"Ah, at last you are awake, we were a little worried," a pair of bright eyes of uncertain colour looked down at Kymar from a tanned, quite handsome face. "Are you feeling better now? You had quite a nasty fall, on to cobbles. And that sword wound in your leg went quite deep, that will take some healing I can tell you. But we will do our best, you'll soon be back on your feet…"

"Who are you? Where am I?" Demanded Kymar suspiciously.

The man smiled kindly, "I am Irator, Brother of the Essence, bestower of the Gift. But please be calm, you will only open your wounds again. You are in hospital, the finest on the island."

Kymar glared at Irator, "You're a Warlock, a dirty soul stealer." She tried to lunge at him but found herself unable to move, her arms and legs restrained by thick leather straps fastened to the frame of a large bed. She kicked and tugged against the straps for some time until Irator spoke again.

"Please, young one, don't struggle, we mean you no harm, have we not saved your life? You would have bled to death if not for our healing skills."

Kymar stopped thrashing, because she wasn't getting anywhere she told herself, not because of anything the Warlock said.

"Why? Why save me just to kill me again? That's what you do isn't it? Rip peoples' souls out, turn them into slaves, I'd sooner be dead."

Irator sighed deeply, a look of utter sadness crossed his face. "You see, that's how you look upon it, as a curse. But if you would only look deeper." He brightened slightly. "How many people have you seen starving to death? How many people have been murdered? Or women died in childbirth? How often have you heard of people being attacked on lonely roads? Do you know what rape is? Ever heard of it?" Irator waited for an answer, Kymar merely shook her head. "You know why, because it never happens," he was in full motion now, passionate about his subject, he began to pace up and down. "There is no crime, no hunger, no greed, nobody more important than anyone else, no taxes, no sickness, no homeless people or orphans. Everyone has enough because no one takes it all. Do you see, our way is the best for all, not just for some? Look around, do you see a palace here, or just a working chapel?"

Kymar looked around the room for the first time. It was fairly large, about three hay wagons long, and two wide. The walls were a yellowish stone, well made but not perfect. In the middle of the room was a strange open coffin-like device, around the edges were neat wooden beds with bright white sheets and brown blankets. All the beds were empty. Kymar noticed they all had straps like the one she was in.

"In this hospital, anyone from anywhere can come here and be treated, but as you see, they are a healthy bunch." Irator gestured with a wide sweep of his arm, grinning proudly.

"Yes, I can see that now, haven't I been foolish," Kymar smiled her best smile, "I am sorry for causing any bother, could I sit up now, have something to eat perhaps, if that's not too much trouble?"

"No, no, that's not any bother, we can have something brought up for you, a light soup I think, to start with anyway." Irator disappeared out of the only door, smiling as he went.

Kymar looked around again, trying to find any other exits or escape routes. When Irator came back several minutes later, she tried to see out of the door, to see what was out there and which way the kitchens were. Plenty of ways out of a kitchen. But all she could see was another room, smaller but similar to the one she occupied.

"There now, a bowl of fresh boltrang soup, some bread and a comb of honey, from the Head Priest's own hives no less." He laid a small table on the bed, table, bowl and spoon were all made of wood. He began to unbuckle the straps on Kymar's arms and legs. When she was free she began to eat rapidly, everything edible quickly disappearing into her mouth. She didn't normally like the sweet melon like vegetables, but this might be her last meal, for a while at least. Irator watched happily as she ate, but for once stayed silent. Kymar licked the last of the honey from the waxy comb, then laid back against the headboard. "Where are my clothes and things? I would hate to lose them."

"Oh, don't worry about that, they have been cleaned and mended, and even now are stacked neatly in this cupboard."

Kymar looked down by her left side at the small wooden cupboard by the bed, too small to contain a sword she thought, a scowl flitting across her face. Irator mis-read her expression bent down and opened the small door. "Look, it's all there as I said."

Kymar glanced in, saw her clothes neatly stacked, but no sword or the leather pouches she used to wear. She forced a smile.

Then sliding one hand under the edge of the table she suddenly lifted it and slammed it against Irator's head. The Warlock staggered backwards as Kymar leapt from the bed. The wooden implements thudded onto the stones, the priest doing much the same moments later. By this time Kymar was half dressed and heading for the door. She glanced around once to make sure he was not following then quietly closed the door behind her. She was gratified to see a lock on the outside with a key in it. She turned the key, removed it and dropped it into a pocket. The outside room had only one door, to the left of the one she had come through. Stealthily she approached it, listened for a few moments, then hearing nothing she stepped out.

The two guards outside the door were mildly surprised to see her, Kymar was shocked but not enough to slow her wits. She put one hand to her forehead and took a small step forwards, pretending to faint. The two guards, being men, immediately leaned forward to catch her. As soon as they moved she stepped back again, throwing out her arms so that her knuckles connected simultaneously with their lower groins. The two guards, being on duty inside the castle and outside the hospital wore only thin garments, no armour at all. Kymar raced away as the two men tried to shout for help, follow Kymar and not cry at the same time.

Kymar was elated at the success, the last of her pounding head melted away as she ran fleet of foot towards the smell of cooking foods.

After several frantic minutes following different odour trails, she finally reached the massive kitchens. The place was overflowing with people, all preparing or cooking foods of different kinds. They mostly ignored her, seemingly intent on the one task they had at hand, cutting, chopping and mixing with a fevered skill. One corner was stacked with crates of vegetables of varying sizes, there was a rack filled with different types of eggs. Bundles of dried herbs hung from the rafters and animals in various states of dismemberment hung everywhere. The smells were almost overpowering, wafts of spicy stews blew from the racks of pots over the fire, fighting with the aroma of roasting flesh from the spits below. Herb smells dropping from the ceiling met the rising odours from the vegetable chopping area.

As Kymar had expected the kitchen contained many exits, the rubbish shoot, a large door to the slaughterhouse and several open windows of various sizes. She selected a door that opened onto an open courtyard through which ran a small stream. The stream disappeared through a large archway out into the green fields beyond. Kymar was just stepping casually over the step when she suddenly remembered Garen.

Chapter Fifteen

Garen was having a strange dream about being sucked into a massive whirlpool. His head was throbbing, he was trying to shout, but everyone seemed to be ignoring him. As he was pulled further into the centre he was getting smaller until a passing mouse was bigger than him. The mouse laughed, "You'll wake up soon enough, then the Brothers will arrive." The voice was very deep, for a mouse.

The water surrounding Garen began to fade to black, then a wide face formed in its place. The face spoke with the voice of the mouse, "Looks like he's awake at last, didn't get hit that hard, must be one of those runts." The face laughed.

Finally the scene in front of Garen resolved itself. The face grew a full body, very full in fact. Behind the fat soldier stood two thinner ones, a man and a woman. Garen was in what was obviously a dungeon; dirty brown stone walls, green moisture dripping from some crack in one corner, a small, high window barred by thick ironwork. And the usual pile of dirty straw to sleep on. The only thing missing was the rats.

The woman pushed her way forwards, the two men fell back without a word.

"I am Krane, Captain of the Peace Keepers, you will tell me now, where the rest of your gang are hiding, what you planned to do and any other information you may have." Krane leaned forward as though to listen to Garen's full confession.

"Er, I'm sorry, it's just the three of us, and we didn't really have a plan, we just came for a look around..."

"You expect me to believe that? Never mind, the Brothers will soon have you talking." She turned to the two men, "Take him to the Chamber of Enlightenment." Krane turned and walked away head high.

The fat soldier walked towards Garen grinning, "You'll like it in there, there are all sorts of games to play, I wish I could come with you."

The thin soldier smiled, "Don't say that Otura, you might get your wish." They both laughed whilst hauling Garen to his feet and dragging him away.

The two soldiers smelled of old sweat, Garen was positioned just right to notice, jammed between them, their armpits on a level with his face. He tried not to breathe, but this proved impossible. So he tried politely not to notice.

After being dragged down several corridors, all very clean and tidy, he was thrown into a large room. Two men grabbed him before he had chance to look around and pulled a soft leather hood over his head. He felt himself being carried across the room then straps tighten around his wrists and ankles, whilst still standing. There was no wall behind him so Garen guessed he was in the middle of the room. A chain began to rattle somewhere to his right, then suddenly he was hoisted up and over until he was left hanging upside down an unknown distance above the ground. His ankles immediately began to ache, his weight pulling painfully against the straps. The hood hung loose around his neck so that he could see light if he looked up, or was it down?

The room then fell silent, Garen was unsure if it was because everyone had left or because someone important had entered. Garen ventured a question, "Hello, what's happening?"

Silence. Garen turned his head, trying to shake off the hood. He realised too late what a silly thing that was to do, he had just woken after being knocked unconscious. His whole head started to spin, he felt his stomach rising. Only the thought of being in a hood full of vomit stopped him throwing up. His ears began to ring, then throb as each heartbeat pulsed; ring, throb, ring, throb. Little black patches appeared in front of his eyes. They danced around, joining hands as they whirled around until they formed one large unconsciousness.

Garen awoke again sometime later, this time he was in a bed, very hard, spartan almost, but still a bed. There were straps on the four corners, but he wasn't restrained. Slowly he looked around. To his right were more beds like the one he was in. At the foot of the bed two men stood grinning down at him, to the left was a door, beyond which stood two soldiers. A small cupboard on long legs was positioned within easy reach of his left hand. A wooden cup, a jug and a wooden platter of hot stew rested on the top. Garen's attention wandered back to the grinning men.

One of them, the taller one, gestured to the bowl. The other, shorter but not as ugly, spoke, "Please eat, you need your strength." Garen was confused, first they knock him out, then they bring him around to torture him, then when he is out again, they bring him around in a bed and feed him. It must be a dream, or a trap. Garen slowly moved his hands together and pinched his skin. It hurt. So, this is a trap then.

"What's the catch, is it drugged? You don't get me that easily."

The better looking of the two approached the bowl and ate a large spoonful. Then, still grinning, placed the platter in front of Garen. "Eat, we are here to help."

Garen looked from one man to the other, then down at the food. He picked up half a spoonful, tasted it, found it not too bad, then ate the rest, after all he needed his strength if he was to escape.

When the last mouthful was slipping down his throat he noticed the shorter man falling asleep on the next bed. Before he could do anything, his eyes grew heavy, his mind began to drift and the blackness returned.

Garen woke to a darkened room. He was surprised to find himself still in the bed, still not strapped in. He also felt a lot better, indeed when he experimentally moved his head, the candle opposite hardly spun at all. There was more food beside his bed, fruits of different kinds, and a jug filled with a sweet milky substance.

"We call that Honeydew, it's very good for a fast recovery."

Out of the darkness came the shorter of the two men who were there earlier. "I am Brother Irator, Brother of the Essence, you have been asleep for almost a full day, but I have been by your side constantly. You will soon recover, there is a lot for you to learn, much of which will come as a surprise to you. But I see you are a strong, intelligent boy, a credit to your father."

"My father," Garen sat up quickly, his heart pounding in his chest." You know my father?"

"Oh yes, well, we do now, we looked you up in the records, we keep everything written down you know. Our methods have remained unchanged for many years. Everything registered and recorded, all in proper order, I'll show you if you like."

"Yes I would like that, and my jar too, I would really like to see that." Garen tried to keep the eagerness out of his voice.

Irator laughed, his jolly face crinkling around the eyes. "I'm sorry, that's not possible, only the Brothers may enter the central chamber. But I can show you the library, that's where we keep all the collected knowledge of generations long gone. It is a truly magnificent sight, books, scrolls, tablets, carvings everywhere you look, all bursting with knowledge, if you know how to read them of course."

"Can we go now? I'll need my clothes." Garen threw back the thin sheets and stood on the cold floor.

Irator grinned widely, "You are keen aren't you. Your clothes have been cleaned, mended and placed in that cupboard."

Garen pulled his clothes out of the long legged cupboard and dressed.

With a suitable escort of what Irator insisted on calling Peace Keepers, he and Garen made their way along several corridors and up several creaking stairways into the library. Garen was suitably impressed by the size of it. He stood open mouthed for several seconds.

Irator interrupted his thoughts, "Here, look Garen, these are your records."

Garen moved over to stand beside Irator, who sat on a long bench worn and polished by many generations of clerical backsides. A massive bookcase ascended behind the bench, every book looked the same, two spans high, three fingers thick, bound in brown hide. Irator was pointing to tiny but neat writing in one of the books. Now, Garen couldn't actually read, but he didn't want Irator to know. He looked to where the Warlock was pointing, noticing his own name in slightly larger black letters. The rest of the writing was just a jumble of lines to Garen.

"Yes, I see, that's very interesting. But the writing is a bit small, my eye's are still a bit blurry from that knock I took. Could you read it out for me?"

Irator looked up at Garen, a small smile at the corners of his mouth. "Yes of course, sit down please."

When Garen was seated to Irator's satisfaction he rested the book on his lap, a serious look on his face. "Now Garen, what I am about to read for you is the truth, you may not like it or even believe it, but you can read it for yourself if you wish, when you're feeling better of course. I assure you we only want what is best for the people of Huclan, I am sure that is your wish too, or you wouldn't be here. Is that not so?"

Garen squirmed uncomfortably on the bench, he didn't like the sound of this one bit, too much responsibility by far. "Well, yes I suppose so. Just read it to me and I'll tell you after." Garen smiled his nicest smile.

"Very well, I will read the parts that are relevant to you, some of it you wouldn't understand, but it in no way changes the meaning of it, is that clear?"

Garen nodded unsurely.

Irator lifted the book until it was very close to his eyes, angling the pages towards an oil lamp, then began to read in a soft, steady voice. "The magic of the Gift was performed on one Garen of Cliffsedge on the day of his birth the eightieth day of spring in the year 211 After Enlightenment... One thirty Day later Brother...noticed the child laughing...other actions...the Gift was bestowed again...Two seasons after the child was observed to be playing happily...Brother Parsathan himself removed the child to the Fort of Souls and performed the rite in the room of Enlightenment...To the surprise of all concerned the child remained free of the Gift. Brother Parsathan thus decreed that a potential successor...Garen would be returned to his home to be raised among his own kind until such a time as he is ready to begin." Irator turned towards a slightly pale looking Garen. "Three times you were given the Gift, three times you resisted it. You are a very special person Garen, not since Parsathan himself has there been one such as you. This is a great honour. Now Brother Parsathan would like to have a little talk with you, explain a few things." Irator stood slowly and carefully replaced the book on the shelf.

Garen sat quietly for a moment, not sure whether to believe what he had heard. Irator gripped his arm and helped him to his feet. "Come on, we mustn't keep Brother Parsathan waiting."

Garen finally found his tongue before the walnut door of Parsathan's study. "You mean all that time I have been evading the soldiers, cleverly hiding and playing dumb you've known all about me?"

"Not everyone, only a few, myself, Brother Parsathan, a few Peace Keepers. But it was necessary for you to see the people as they are, so you are able to understand better what will be asked of you. Now, stand up straight, smarten up your clothes, that's it."

Irator knocked loudly on the door, then walked straight in. "Brother Parsathan, a visitor for you". Irator allowed Garen into the room then pushed him gently forwards with a hand on his back.

Behind the large desk at one end of the room stood the other man Garen had seen grinning at him in the hospital.

"I am very sorry for your treatment earlier, we didn't know you had arrived until Brother Krane brought you to my attention. I trust you are feeling better?"

Garen shuffled his feet, looking down at the bare floor, then remembering Sciel and Kymar he looked Parsathan in the eye. "Where are my friends? You'll get no favours from me unless they are safe."

"You're friends are perfectly safe," Parsathan didn't actually know where they were at the moment, but he was almost sure they were safe. "Nothing to worry about, and you haven't heard what I have to say yet. At least give me time for that."

"I know what you want, you want me to take over when you're dead, you being dead I can live with, the other part is out."

Parsathan almost laughed, "I am sorry young man but you seem to have been misinformed." He looked at Irator, who simply smiled. "Come over here and sit down, I will try and explain it to you properly."

Garen walked nervously to the indicated chair and sat down on the front edge. Parsathan leaned nearer to Garen, his hands flat against the desk. "Brother Irator has explained to you about how special you are, leaving out certain details, at my request. You understand that a successor is needed to take over my duties when I retire. Now, all of the Brothers have been given the Gift, including Brother Irator. His resistance was very high but not high enough to allow his promotion to Head Priest. The person selected must be, as you have gathered, completely immune to the effects of the Gift, for obvious reasons. But that person must also be trained by myself in the disciplines of priesthood, from a very early age. You Garen are too old."

"So why didn't you hang onto me when I was a child? and why does my father think he kept me safe all these years?"

"That was a risk I decided to take. One child may later turn out to be unsuitable, be sickly or not very bright. But several children, all fighting for this chair would soon weed out the spindly growth. Besides I wasn't ready to retire then, not that I am now, but we must be ready." Parsathan sat down in his high backed chair, was quiet for a few moments. "Your father is a good man, Garen, we gave you back to him and he was happy. We told him that if you showed signs of becoming a Wild One he was to inform us immediately. The order was only spoken, not strong enough to compel your father to act. So when you showed signs of rebellion he simply hid you away. Whatever he has told you about those days is true, at least in his mind.

Garen looked suspiciously at Parsathan, "Then what do you want me for?"

"I am sure the task you perform will be one you enjoy immensely, a young man such as yourself. You see, it's long been known that children receive certain features from their parents; hair colour, eyes, facial features, and so on. We believe that given the right women you could father a child, or even several, with your inner strength, children who could be trained to the priesthood..."

Garen had stood very slowly, his leg muscles seeming to contract on their own. His face was as pale as a ghost.

"Now there is no need to worry about a thing, we will give you quarters here, provide you with all you need to keep your strength up. We can bring the women in groups so you can choose your favourite, what do you say?"

Garen remained standing, swaying slightly, for several moments. Then he did what any inexperienced sixteen year old would have done when faced with such an offer. He ran for it. Brother Irator tried to catch him but Garen dodged skilfully past him and disappeared out of the door.

"Let him go Brother, he needs time to himself to think over what he needs to do. I'm sure he'll be back. Inform the guards to leave him in peace, but not to let him out of this block."

Parsathan returned to a thick tome that had been open on his desk.

"Is that wise Brother Parsathan? He may try to do something foolish."

"Nonsense Brother, what could one young boy get up to in a fort full of Peace Keepers?"

Brother Irator quietly left, softly closed the walnut door, then ran speedily off to find a messenger.

Chapter Sixteen

Sciel was in hell. First he thought it was heaven, everywhere he turned there was food of all kinds just sitting waiting to be eaten. When he had casually walked over to one of the laden carts he had been driven away by shouting stall owners brandishing sticks. He didn't understand humans at all, they had all that food, yet they seemed to be swapping it for bits of metal. Even I can't eat metal, he thought.

Sciel didn't understand time, so he wasn't sure how much time had gone by since his friend and the strange girl had been captured. It had got dark once or twice, he knew that. He also knew he had only eaten seven meals in that time, that's the same as fingers on both hands less one. Starving wasn't the word for it, his stomach felt like it would never be full again.

As darkness fell Sciel found a quiet corner by a warm chimney on a flat roof. He had spent most of his time in the castle on one roof or another, since he had been chased up here by the soldiers. He laughed to himself as he remembered the looks on their faces as he had ran straight up a vertical stone wall. He doubted whether he could do it again, at least not until his claws grew back.

Sciel vowed to find his friend, rescue him, then go back to their old life in the forest, clowning around, finding food. A cool wind began to blow off the mountains, making him shiver. Before, the wind had been warmer, blowing from the land. This new wind brought with it a familiar odour, one he had not smelled in a long time. He got to his feet, padding cautiously in the direction his nose told him. On one side of the roof, just below the parapet, a vent opening spilled out a warm, yeasty odour. It was very strong, to a Teff completely unmistakable, it was the smell of other Teff.

Sciel was so excited he almost fell off the roof leaning over to trace the vent. A slight bulge in the stonework showed it running straight down the wall towards an iron grille set into the wall, its lower edge level with the ground.

Sciel quickly found a way down, then sneaked cautiously towards the grille. The odour was very strong now, the mixed smell of several Teff, male and female. He quietly edged up to the bars, his ears alert for the sounds of soldiers. Sciel looked in through the grille. It was set high on the wall of a round room like a wide well. The floor was deep with straw. Opposite his viewpoint was a narrow door, wooden at the bottom, iron bars at the top. On the same side as the arm Sciel threw stones with were the Teff, huddled together. He hissed softly, then a little louder. Some of the Teff stirred but didn't awake.

"Oy! You lot, are you asleep or what?" Sciel said in Teff, a series of growling words that sounded like a dog talking.

A head lifted from the pack, its body lost in the huddle.

"What do you want youngster? Trying to get in here? Just keep making that noise, you soon will be."

"What are you doing in there? Shall I rescue you?"

The head laughed, "If you want to try, you're welcome, but don't blame me when you get yourself killed. Now shut up, we're trying to sleep."

Sciel was puzzled by the attitude of the other Teff, surely they didn't want to stay in there? Perhaps they had given up hope. All they needed was a bit of a shove to get them going, like someone unlocking the door. Sciel suddenly thought of his friend, perhaps the Teff would help him rescue Garen, if he could just find him.

Sciel stealthily made his way along the base of the wall looking for a way in. Just around the next corner Sciel found what he was looking for, rather more than that in fact. The door was massive, obviously the entrance for horses and coaches. Indeed it smelled of all kinds of beasts, it was also shut tight.

Sciel crept up to the door sniffing quietly, all the odours mixing together the nearer he got. The smell of humans made him pause for a moment, but he could hear nothing. The door was at least five times as high as Sciel, a good long leap wide, and made from solid wood. There was a small gap at the bottom, but not enough to allow him to crawl under.

Sciel was racking his brain trying to think of a way in when it suddenly became obvious, what did humans do to get through a door? He knocked loudly on the door. After several minutes nothing had happened so he tried again. He was just about to knock a third time when the sound of keys jangling and a grumbling human voice could be heard. The keys rattled in the lock, then a small door Sciel hadn't noticed opened in the larger door. A lantern swung through the door on the end of a thick arm, a gruff voice shouted, "Hello, who's there? Come forward and be identified."

Sciel realised with a start the large flaw in his plan. His mouth opened but nothing came out. His heart beat faster, his mouth became dry. I'm not very good at thinking, he thought, especially not quickly. The figure spoke again, pushing the small door flat open. "Who is it out there? Come forward, or I'll call the guard."

Sciel noticed that the circle of light created by the lantern didn't reach him. So he did what he seemed best at these days, he ran away. As he ran he noticed a tall wooden structure next to the gate. Sciel made his way towards it, then climbed up on top of it, lying down on its flat roof. He heard the human shout and swear for a while, then heard the gate locking.

Sciel lay on his back, watching the clouds float across the crescent of moon. I must try to remember humans can't see very well in the dark, he thought. They can't smell very well either, in fact it's a wonder they get anywhere with those…

He stiffened as the sound of voices came again from behind the door. This time there were several, all grumbling and complaining. The keys jangled and the door swung open, banging back against the larger door. Sciel peered over the edge, three soldiers had emerged and were stamping noisily around, as if to make any intruders think there were a lot of them. The human with the lantern walked out of the door, swinging the light around. The humans peered into the darkness.

Sciel realised the door was wide open, with none of the humans close to it. He stood quickly, jumped silently to the ground, then scampered towards the door. With his back to the wood he crept along watching the humans. His fingers felt along the rough timber, searching for the opening. One of the soldiers turned around, looking towards the human with the lantern.

"You say someone knocked on the door then ran off? Why would anyone do that then?"

"Yes, it does seem strange, you sure you didn't dream it?" added another.

"Of course I didn't dream it, I was wide awake."

"Smell his breath, bet he's been on the jug again."

Sciel was pressed flat against the door, unsure whether to run in or away. He was placed between the light of the lantern and the soldiers, so the humans couldn't see him. But sooner or later they would move. He took a deep breath and dashed in through the door.

"Hey! What was that?" shouted one of the soldiers.

The man with the lantern turned quickly. The three soldiers burst out laughing, "Jumping at shadows again, Artera, don't forget to look under your bed tonight."

The three soldiers could still be heard laughing some minutes later as they made their way back to the guardhouse. The man with the lantern wandered back in, carefully locked the door, then walked off mumbling, "Shadows can't knock on doors can they…all be murdered in our beds…"

When all was again quiet, Sciel emerged cautiously from behind a large crate. Looking around he noticed a wide door that lead in the right direction. The door creaked loudly when he pulled it sending a shiver down his spine. No sound of footsteps could be heard when he listened, so he carried on. The door led onto a stone paved corridor covered with straw. The smell of all the animals the humans kept assailed his nostrils, the smell of Teff drowned under the odorous cacophony. Sciel was certain he knew where the

Teff were, it was just a matter of getting the door open and rousing them to his cause.

Sciel made his way along the corridor, passing horses on one side and sleeping dogs on the other. He was approaching what he thought was the Teff prison, he remembered the half wood half metal gate, when he stood on something under the straw.

He managed to muffle an "Ouch!" with his long hands pressed against his face. He froze on the spot, a thought swum slowly through his head, 'what am I doing?' He slowly scanned the cages, some of the horses were stirring, but they were no threat. The dogs were snoring still.

Sciel's heart was in his throat as he moved on to the next cell. He was feeling very lonely now, stuck in the dungeons of a castle without a friend, surrounded by enemies. His one last hope was the other Teff in the cell.

The door was barred by a heavy plank of wood, Sciel was sure he could move it. He looked around and found a few loose roots dropped by the other animals. His stomach rumbled loudly looking at them, so he ate some, then threw some at the Teff.

The Teff jumped up in alarm, milling around, standing on each other. The noise was quieted down by the Teff Sciel had spoken to earlier. He made sure all was calm, then looked at Sciel.

"Well, I guess you made it then, aren't you going to let us out and lead us to freedom?" his voice, even in whisper, was mocking.

"I'll let you out, but you must promise to do something for me. My friend is being held somewhere in here, I want to rescue him."

"Who is this friend? If he was Teff he would be in here with us." He looked at the others, "any of you this youngsters friend?"

The others mumbled and grumbled, some simply saying no, others being more forceful.

"My friend is human," whispered Sciel through clenched teeth, "he's been more of a friend than anyone else."

The Teff began to get noisy, and were again shushed by the leader. "So, the deal is, you let us out, we help you rescue your friend, and if he's dead already, we still get to leave?"

Sciel was taken aback by the suggestion that Garen might already be dead, he quickly pushed the thought from his mind.

"I will let you out if you help me, whatever the final outcome." Sciel said bravely.

The Teff huddled together for a few minutes, discussing the deal. Then the leader spoke. "Right, let us out, we'll see what we can do. My name is Leafen." He reached through the bars and touched the tip of Sciel's nose, Sciel did the same back.

Sciel was ecstatic, he rushed to the plank and heaved. The plank didn't budge an inch. He looked into the cage, Leafen smiled, "We've tried that."

Sciel pushed again was all his might willing the plank to move. To come this far and then fail was infuriating. Sciel stopped, slumped against the door and sagged to the floor. Several whispered comments about his parentage were made, Leafen remained silent. Sciel looked up at the plank above his head. Underneath was a small recess, in the recess sat a lever as thick as his thumb. Sciel jumped up and began probing the recess. The lever moved under his fingers, but nothing happened. He tried again pulling, pushing, twisting, each time trying to lift the plank. Nothing happened.

Heartened by the certainty that this lever somehow opened the door, Sciel tried again, every way he could think of. He examined the lever, then the plank, then the door. Leafen was watching him intensely, the other Teff had lost interest.

On examining the door frame Sciel noticed that the L-shaped bracket holding the plank wasn't attached to the frame but the plank! Of course, humans knew how tricky Teff were, they couldn't simply bar the door, they had to make sure it couldn't be opened from the inside. Sciel fumbled with the lever again, finding it pulled down, then across, he then pulled the plank. The door, plank, and the brackets that were supposed to be holding it closed, swung outwards as one piece. The look on the faces of the other Teff were worth everything he'd been through. Leafen simply smiled, patting Sciel on the head as he walked past.

"I knew you could do it, youngster, now, which way?"

Sciel wasn't really sure which way to go. He knew how he had got in, so he lead them back down the stone corridor. At the end of the corridor Sciel stopped to listen, the Teff lined up silently behind. They seemed very uncertain of themselves now they were out of the cell, looking nervously around, hanging on to each other. Sciel wasn't sure they would be any use to him, but he guessed they would at least provide extra pairs of eyes. Luckily, Leafen was different, he was sharp and alert without being edgy. Sciel was sure he could count on him, perhaps he would even take over. Sciel was never the type to lead.

When he heard nothing, Sciel leaned around the open door and looked around. Everything was dark, no sign of the soldiers or the lantern man, their odours were fading nicely. He gestured for the Teff to follow, then crept out towards the large door. As soon as the Teff saw the weak moonlight under the door they made a dash towards it, running up and down in front of it, pushing and pulling at every plank, making enough noise to raise even humans.

Sciel panicked, he shouted at Leafen, "No! Stop them, it's locked, we can't get out that way. Come on, this way!"

Sciel picked a door at random and ran towards it. A sudden noise made him stop. Slowly he turned around, not at all liking what he heard.

The metallic sound of chain running over gears filled the air. A slow rumbling noise joined it as the huge door began to rise upwards. The whole castle seemed to vibrate, the dogs started to bark, the Teff yelled in triumph. Sciel slapped his hands to his face in horror. His eyes fell on Leafen who stood to one side of the door turning a wooden wheel. Sciel's wide eyes darted towards the Teff, who were squeezing through the widening gap, then back to Leafen.

"Sorry, youngster, my loyalties are to the Teff, not humans, look after yourself, no hard feelings." He smiled, a genuine warm smile. "We'll meet again you and I, you have a lot to learn."

With that he ducked under the steadily rising door and disappeared into the night.

A light appeared under a door, then another. From a staircase came the sound of booted feet running. Many voices were raised in anger, some promising death and worse to whomever was responsible. Sciel was paralysed with indecision, should he run off with the Teff or stay to help Garen? But the Teff were already out of sight, so that left only one choice. As a door opened and yellow light swung into the room Sciel leapt upwards, grabbed a rope hanging down from the roof, then clambered up into the rafters.

The room below him filled with humans. Soldiers half dressed in leather armour, swords or maces in hand. Watchmen with lanterns or candles. Grooms and stable hands rushed to calm the animals, some shouting for quiet, others offering treats and soothing words. Another human entered, he was dressed in what Sciel called "jumas", with a coat over the top. This and the shiny boots marked him as someone important.

Sciel didn't stay around to see what happened, in the wall opposite he noticed a small, ragged hole leading into another room. He managed to squeeze through, only because he was starving he thought to himself. The room was an unoccupied attic bedroom, with an old bed in pieces in the middle. A narrow chimney was set into the wall at the far end. There was a door, but Sciel decided he'd had enough of those for one day. So, again squeezing himself through, he emerged from the chimney onto a flat roof. The roof looked familiar, indeed one chimney along he found the very place he had settled down in that same night.

Chapter Seventeen

Two soldiers walked slowly past a large water barrel stood in a corner of the empty mess hall. They were talking softly about the prominent features of a certain lady, so didn't notice the crouched figure behind the barrel. When they had safely gone by, Kymar stepped out and carried on her exploration of the castle.

She had nearly left the castle building when she had remembered Garen. So she had turned around and walked back through the kitchens. Unfortunately the door she went back through had looked like the door she first come in by. Kymar had intended to make her way back to the hospital, hoping to find Garen there. She had fell unconscious before Garen, so was unaware of his state of health. But something told her he would have put up a fight, even if it would have been ineffective. She had seen how the soldiers treated her kind, so was in no doubt of their response. If the hospital proved empty, the dungeons would have been her next stop. Now, instead she seemed to be in the soldiers' barracks, not a good place to be at all. Kymar was on her way back to the kitchen when she heard voices. The only place to hide in the whole room had been behind the barrel, which was at the far end of the long hall.

It had occurred to Kymar that the dungeons would be near the soldiers quarters; easier to keep an eye on the prisoners for one thing. The door at the far end of the hall away from the kitchen was open just enough for Kymar to see through. She put one eye to the gap, listening at the same time. The thin beam of light shining through the gap lit a wedge of dark corridor. Set in the wall opposite was a wooden door with a barred opening. The floor was stone, well worn, slightly dirty. From the look of the door this must be the prison cells, thought Kymar. A quick search will tell me if Garen is here. If so I can always come back.

Kymar opened the door, spreading light across the passage. The rest of the passage was in total darkness to Kymar's eyes. She stepped through, then closed the door behind her. With her back to the door and one hand on the handle Kymar stood still for a few moments to let her eyes adjust to the dark. When she could see enough, although not very well, she picked a direction then slowly made her way along the passage. Her left hand kept in constant contact with the rough, slightly damp, stone wall. This place was certainly dungeon like, although to Kymar's mind it seemed at odds with the rest of the building, as though someone had installed the damp and the shadows deliberately. She had certainly seen no other signs of either anywhere else.

A noise up ahead made Kymar press flat against the wall. Some way further on a burning torch appeared followed by a figure. Heavy footsteps echoed flatly along the passage. The torch cast long shadows across the face and shoulders of the figure, distorting its features, stretching its nose and chin to monstrous proportions. Glints of yellow flashed off the metal studs and off the sharpened edge of the helm the figure wore. No doubting the apparel of a soldier. Kymar looked behind then back at the figure, deciding what to do. Soldiers in ones and twos were easy enough to handle, more than that she wasn't so certain of. She was so close to the cells it seemed a pity to turn back now.

As the figure neared, Kymar, who had been hidden by the darkness, stepped into the middle of the passage. The soldier stopped, seemingly unsurprised. The shadowed face looked Kymar over for a moment, then started to draw a weapon. But Kymar had learned not to hesitate, size up the opposition fast, then move. In the semi-darkness Kymar's shadow suddenly grew as she leapt towards the soldier. The torch remained steady in the hand of the soldier despite the approaching danger. The soldier's other hand was pulling out a wooden club when Kymar made contact. She grabbed the soldier by the shoulders, glared into the light and dark eyes and swiftly lifted her knee between leather-clad legs.

As bone connected with bone, as the shock jarred up

and down her leg, Kymar's eyes filled with recognition. The vision travelled towards her brain. As it arrived a heavy blow knocked her head against the soldiers armour. A metal stud drove deep into her forehead. The shadows mingled, then darkened in a whirl of black. Kymar's last thought faded into silence, 'damn, a woman…'

* * * *

Once again vivid dreams crashed through Kymar's head. A long tunnel like a giant burrow stretched out in front of her. Up ahead a military band played the loudest tune they knew very badly. Behind, a massive light shone so brightly that the reflections from the oversized instruments lanced her eyes with pain. On and on they marched, the light getting brighter, and the band getting louder the worse they played. Kymar pressed her hands to her ears and yelled for silence. Suddenly the tunnel was filled with water and the band washed past her, clutching their instruments to stay afloat. The icy tidal wave smacked into her, taking her breath, making her shudder, pounding her against the wall. The light wavered then went out. The tunnel was empty, at the end a candelabrum stuck out of the wall. The sides of the tunnel peeled back, revealing a room shaped like a cube. Kymar realised she was lying on her back looking up at the ceiling. Slowly she lifted her head, expecting the worst.

There it stood, grinning back at her. She tried to get up but couldn't move. Looking around Kymar found that she was fastened ankle and wrist inside a shallow coffin like structure.

"Let me go you grinning idiot, or I'll…"

"Now my dear, please be calm, I know you will thank me after." Said the tall man, still smiling. "My name is Parsathan, Head Priest, you have met Brother Irator of course."

Irator rose from a chair and walked around to Kymar's left side.

"I hope you are well dear, that leg wound is healing

fast, but then you have been asleep for some time. Don't worry about that bump on the head you gave me, no damage done there, not to my brain anyway. It's my own fault really, should have known you were a little wary, in a new place and all that. You don't need to worry about that temper either, we will soon have that fixed."

"What are you going to do?" said Kymar a little worriedly.

Parsathan smiled, "Well, we are going to give you the Gift of course, we will be so pleased to release you from your troublesome temper. Then you can go home with a nice little family we have found for you, they never had children of their own. Wouldn't that be good?" He grinned again, even wider.

Kymar lowered her head onto the coffin and laughed, she was so relieved. Irator and Parsathan exchanged glances, Parsathan approached Kymar's right side. "Whatever is so amusing child?"

She lifted her head up, still laughing, "You really are a grinning idiot aren't you? You haven't got a clue."

"I'm sorry my dear but we don't understand. The giving of the Gift isn't usually greeted with such levity."

"You've already tried, it didn't work then, it won't work now. So let me out of this box before I have to break something." She glared meaningfully at Parsathan's nose.

Parsathan and Irator withdrew to the other side of the room to hold a whispered discussion. Kymar tried to loosen her bonds while their backs were turned, without success. A few moments later they both returned, taking up position either side.

"We think we have worked out what you mean my dear," explained Parsathan in his best patronising voice. "You think that the Gift spell has been used on you before, and didn't work is that right?"

"Of course, what did you think I meant?" Kymar said sharply.

Irator leant over, "We have searched our records very carefully, there is no record of you at all."

"Good, that's the way I like it. I don't want to be catalogued in any books of yours, soul stealer!"

"Every time the Gift is bestowed…" began Irator

"Ripped you mean, ripped out of the living body by a blood sucking Warlock! Get away from me, go on, get out of my sight before I rip your souls out the hard way!" Kymar was yelling now, thrashing her arms and legs as far as the straps would allow.

Parsathan and Irator stepped back a few paces. They let her shout and thrash until she had worn herself out.

Kymar was scared. What had she done? These two seemed so confident. The bindings wouldn't move. Had she got herself into deep trouble?

"Now you have quietened down I will try to explain what I said earlier." Irator stepped in closer again, Parsathan stayed where he was. "Every time the spell is cast a record is written in a small book. On the return of the Brother to the fort the book is copied out into the larger books. Every time. It's part of the spell, no record written means no spell. So you see child, if your name isn't in the record, you have never been Gifted."

Kymar was in a state of panic, she was trying to remember her mother's actual words, the times she had told her about the Warlocks, about the spell, about her soul being stolen. She had said they had tried, did that mean tried with the spell or tried to find her? An image of her mother formed in her head, she was speaking, about her father. The image wouldn't keep still, she tried again, concentrating on the face she knew so well.

"… I kept them from you, I wouldn't let them take you, we had to hide, hide still, until someone kills the Warlocks…"

A strange chanting filled the air, the words seemed to buzz in her head. Looking up she saw Irator holding a Soul jar, carefully removing the top, placing it on a table above her head. Her mind froze, her body went limp. Over and over in her head the phrase repeated, '…I kept them away from you…I kept them away from you…'

Chapter Eighteen

Garen had been wandering around the castle for sometime. At first he had done his best to avoid the guards, but had soon realised they weren't interested in him. Except for the time he had stumbled across a small door with a peephole view of the stables. He had yanked it open and dashed through straight into the arms of a large soldier. Then he had been unceremoniously dumped back inside. It seemed they had been told to keep him inside, nothing more.

Garen took quick advantage of the situation, making himself familiar with the castle. Walking around, trying to get back to where he had started by going a different route, He soon discovered several things; a lot of the corridors and stairs looked identical, but were in actual fact slightly different. A slightly different tapestry here, different shaped handrails there, and so on. Once you knew it was fairly simple. Also, the staff who worked in the castle, maids, cooks, stable boys etc. had all been Ripped. The only free people were most, not all, of the soldiers and the Brothers.

Garen had decided now would be the best time to find the Soul jars. When he had asked Irator about the jars the Brother had said something about a central chamber, and his eyes had momentarily flicked upwards when he spoke. Garen found a wide window on the inside wall of the castle and counted the storeys. There was one more above him than there should have been. But he could find no stairs, ladders or anything.

Garen had also been talking to some of the castle dwellers. Most either knew nothing or weren't saying. But some of the soldiers liked to gossip. He had heard that a wild young woman was at large in the castle after severely injuring two guards.

Garen was in no doubt of whom they were speaking. He expected to run into her at any moment. He had also

- 75 -

heard of an escape by some of the animals in the stables. It seems someone had captured some Teff somehow, but they had finally escaped, every last one. The hunters had tracked the Teff as far as the forested hill below the castle where they simply disappeared. Garen smiled to himself at this news, Sciel was safe so he no longer had to worry about his friend.

All this thinking and exploring had so far kept his mind off the things Parsathan had said. He wasn't absolutely sure it sounded so bad, but his intelligence told him it must be. After all they came here to free the souls, not allow the regime to continue.

To occupy himself and keep him out of the way of the guards, Garen had decided to find the stairs up to the top floor, how ever long it took. To this end he was now secreted in an alcove behind a large marble statue. The view from behind the horse sculpture allowed him to see a considerable distance in two directions.

Garen was getting stiff joints with the waiting when a Brother suddenly appeared about fifty paces in front to his left. Garen had only looked away for a few seconds, but there he was as if he had risen up out of the floor. Garen waited for him to walk off then quickly approached the spot where he thought the Brother had appeared. He had examined the walls all the way around this section of the castle, finding nothing unusual. Garen wished Sciel was here, he could open almost anything. Now of course he realised he'd been looking in the wrong place.

Garen paced along the wall, tapping the floor until he found a hollow sounding panel. The panel looked like the rest of the wood planked floor, dark wood polished by generations of parlour maids and Brothers leather boots. On hands and knees, Garen felt around the floor until he found a thin seam. It was extremely close to the wall, at first he didn't believe that he'd found it.

After a few minutes of scrambling about he finally got the panel open. It hinged back to reveal a very narrow opening, just wide enough for a man to enter with his back to the wall.

Garen listened for a few moments, he didn't know what for, he'd just seen Sciel do it. With his back against the wall he walked sideways down into the hole. With one last look around he closed the panel after him. Stone steps led down and around, into the castle wall, then up a ridiculously narrow stairway. It was so narrow Garen had to walk like a crab all the way, wondering how some of the bigger Brothers got in. At the top was a normal looking door, which opened inwards.

The door swung quietly on its hinges at Garen's touch. His first look through the door made him freeze. A fully armoured soldier holding the biggest sword Garen had ever seen stood to attention before a large shed like box. At first Garen thought the soldier was ignoring him like the rest. But when the soldier didn't move an inch, not even a twitch, Garen looked closer.

The soldier was a wooden frame with armour on, topped by a wax head. The hands were similar, moulded around the hilt of the sword. When Garen closed the door he found another on the other side. Garen wondered if these were replacements for the real thing. There hadn't been a threat to the rulers here for many years, the real ones must have been given duty elsewhere.

Examining the rest of the room Garen realised there was no other way out. The stone walls enclosed an area as big as a small cottage, with the two boxes against the walls. a small window above each box let in dull sunlight. Something clicked in Garen's head, his eyes lit up and he marched confidently up to one of the soldiers. He smiled up at the tall figure then ducked behind it, through the box and into a long room.

Not for the first time in the last few weeks, Garen's mouth dropped open. He stared in wonder at the rows and rows of shelves, all neatly stacked with Soul jars. Garen wandered down the centre of the room, which carried on around the castle. As he walked he tried to calculate the number of Soul jars actually kept here. The jars were stacked nine wide by five deep on each shelf. There were nine shelves from floor to ceiling in each block with the same again on the other side of the room. The blocks were grouped together in threes. Garen could see at least twenty groups of three on either side of the room, with more disappearing around a corner out of sight. Counting on his fingers Garen worked out there were several thousand Soul jars here. He had given up trying to be accurate after nine times five, times nine, times three.

Garen approached one of the shelves and carefully removed a jar. He turned the red clay cylinder over in his hands. The cylinder was as high as both of his hands, as thick around as a drinking cup and sealed at both ends with a wide clay tablet as thick as his thumb. When he tried to scratch the clay he found it very hard, his fingernail not leaving a mark. On what he took to be the front was a series of imprinted characters, like small pictures made with straight lines. Garen stroked the jar gently for a few moments, then placed it back on the shelf.

A strange noise had slowly been building up in Garen's ears, a chanting sound, getting louder as he walked around the room. He shook his head but the sound persisted. At the midway point the room broadened slightly. On what would have been the outside wall was, instead, a screened wall. The bottom half of the wall was normal stone but the top half was a screen intricately carved with ivies and other climbing plants. The droning chant came from beyond the screen.

Cautiously Garen approached the screen, which appeared to writhe as the torchlight from the room beyond swelled and darkened. Garen's breath caught in his mouth as all at once the scene below played out on his senses.

Kymar was strapped in a shallow coffin. Irator was ripping her soul from her body whilst Parsathan stood by. A heat haze was rising from Kymar. A Soul jar stood open at her head. The lid to the jar was in Irator's hand. Garen tried to shout but a voice in his head told him not to. She was safe, they had tried before and failed, just like they had done to him. But then what was the heat rising? What if they had made a new, stronger spell? What if it wasn't that spell but some other? A death spell for instance. His voice burst from his mouth. An incoherent cry echoed off the walls.

Parsathan looked up suddenly, hesitated a moment, then rushed from the room. Irator didn't even pause in his chanting. Garen watched in horror as the haze began to flow like honey into the jar. Kymar, her eyes open, physically slumped as the spell tore part of her soul away and trapped it within the jar. Irator slapped the lid in place with one hand, wrapped a sealing strip around it with the other then stepped back smiling.

Garen beat his fists uselessly against the screen. For all its intricacy it was carved out of stone three fingers thick. He turned and ran, looking wildly around for something heavy. The only things in here were Soul jars and shelves. He didn't really like the idea of using someone's soul as a battering ram and the shelves were fastened solidly to floor and ceiling.

He made his way back through the boxes, down the stairway and around the passage. The panel wouldn't move, as if something heavy had been placed on top. In panic he turned around, scraping bare skin as he rushed up the narrow stairs. Back in the first room he wrestled one of the large swords from the wax soldier, ripping its hand off with it. Garen ran down the room, his breath shallow but rapid. The sword was heavy, but he hardly noticed his muscles straining.

Garen swung the sword with all his might at the stone screen. His hands above and below the wax hand made for a strange sight, as though he was being aided by some ghostly figure. The sword slammed against the stone with a metallic ring and a shower of dust. Several times Garen repeated the attack. When he stopped to examine the screen, his breath rasping in his lungs, he saw very little damage had been done. Worse still, the room below was empty.

With a yell Garen launched himself across the room towards the screen, sword held point first in front of him. He barely managed to keep the giant blade high enough to hit the stone. As it struck Garen's weight carried it on forwards. The blade jammed in the wall, flexed alarmingly, then snapped. The rest of the sword flicked upwards, continuing on, driven by Garen's enraged energy. The broken tip crashed into the screen, slewing sideways. His chest collided with the rounded hilt levering the sword further into the stone, finally knocking his wind out.

Lower down the wall, the ragged end of the broken blade was driven into Garen's upper leg by his forward momentum. He looked down at the strange sensation, pulling his leg back to get a better look. Until recently Garen had suffered little pain in his life, at the moment it looked like he was catching up. The rushing fire of agony spread up and down his leg. Only his anger and panic kept him conscious. He managed to hang onto the hilt lodged in the screen as the pain swelled, then fell to a dull torment.

He decided the only thing to do was be brave, pull out the blade, then carry on. Kymar could have been taken anywhere by now. So, Garen gritted his teeth, gripped the blade and pulled. The shard came out but he cut his hands doing it. He channelled the pain into anger at his own stupidity. Why hadn't he used a cloth or something?

Garen calmed himself enough to tend to his wounds, which thankfully weren't as bad as they looked. The cut on his hand soon stopped after a little pressure, the leg wound required a more serious remedy. He tore a sleeve from his shirt and tied it around the wound, which thankfully stopped bleeding. Ignoring the pulsing in his leg, Garen once again turned his attention to the screen.

The sword had lodged solidly in the stone. On closer inspection Garen saw cracks through some of the thinner carvings. Quickly, trying to ignore his pain, he wrenched the sword back and forth with all his might until it came free. Several of the carvings were now cracked, some actually broken off. Garen plunged the sword into a different part of the screen and tried again. The thinner carvings gave way under his onslaught.

Soon the screen had a large hole through it, but as soon as he tried to climb through a familiar voice sounded behind.

"There you are young man. It wasn't really necessary to break that was it? It was very old you know. Come, let me explain a few things to you."

Garen leaned through the hole, looking back through the screen. Parsathan and two large soldiers stood in the room. Those soldiers didn't come up those stairs that's for sure, thought Garen as he slipped through the hole.

His fall into the room was broken by a bed, unfortunately someone had removed the mattress. He slammed into the wood, smashed it to kindling, then hit the mattress which had been put on the floor underneath.

Garen leapt to his feet and ran unsteadily out of the room, picking splinters out of his palms. He ran wildly down a corridor, passing a door he recognised, this was the hospital wing. Garen tried to think as he ran, where would they have taken Kymar? Out of the castle for sure, away from Garen. They wouldn't leave any reminders to distract him from the job in hand. They would probably take her out of the main gate, it was much quicker than any other way. The sun shone through the gate at noon, so he headed towards sunlight.

A sudden thought halted Garen in his tracks, what good could he do Kymar now? It was her Soul jar he needed. He turned on his heels and raced back towards the hospital. The images of the jars he had seen on the shelves crowded to the front of his head. They had been the same at both ends; a cylinder with a thick cap sealed in place. The one Irator had was sealed with a waxy cloth. Sometime between the spell being cast and the jar going on the shelf it had to be sealed properly. Where would they do that? Somewhere close at a guess, to do a quick job.

Dashing around like a mad man, Garen barged into every room he went by on the way back to the hospital. Finding nothing he carried on past the room he had broken into, hunting ever more feverishly. Several Brothers looked up at him as he entered some of the rooms, a few soldiers hid things behind their backs, but no one stopped him. Garen was struck by how empty the castle was, he had expected it to be teaming with soldiers and Brothers. Obviously numbers weren't important when the population were all mindless puppets.

He pushed a door open and looked inside, was about to move on when he saw a Brother leaving by another door. The Brother turned, slightly startled by the thumping of the door. It was Irator, clutching a Soul jar. Irator carried on through the door, letting it swing shut behind him. Garen rushed after him, catching up with Irator in the next room. The room had a similar door in the opposite wall, which Irator was walking swiftly towards. The room was empty apart from a nervous looking Brother on his way somewhere with a sack, who had pressed himself flat against the wall on seeing Garen's eyes.

"Now Garen, it won't do you any good," said Irator, his voice level. He was clutching the jar to his body with one hand, the other was held out towards Garen, palm out. "Kymar is better off, you know that. Look at the life she'll have, no hunger, no…"

"Spare me the lecture, Brother. I've heard it all before. Give me the jar or I will take it." He advanced on Irator.

"Listen, do you know what will happen if you break the jar? It's not that simple you know, the soul could go anywhere. If the person it was taken from isn't close enough it could go anywhere."

"Kymar is close enough, she couldn't have gone far yet."

"True," Irator conceded. He turned the jar in his hands, examining the markings on the surface. "But you should still…"

Garen was running out of patience, his anger, bubbling under the surface, rose again. He lifted his leg and kicked the jar out of Irator's hands. Three pairs of eyes watched the jar sail into the air, bounce lightly off the ceiling, then land with a dull thud on the floor. The jar vibrated slightly, tapping a rhythm against the wood. Irator rushed over to the jar, picked it up and carefully examined it. A few moments later he smiled.

"These things are very strong you know, Garen. The soul is a tough little thing, any ordinary jar would just break. And the seals have to be strong too." He turned suddenly, heading for the door, "I'll just take this for safe keeping."

Until then Garen had stood motionless, expecting the jar to burst open at any moment. He moved towards Irator. A flash of movement caught his eye, before he could react the other Brother, on a signal from Irator, leapt on Garen. They hit the floor in a tangle of clothes and limbs. The Brother was heavy but wasn't attacking him in any way, just delaying him. Garen lay on his back with his head pinned down by the Brother's chest. One half of his face was covered by clothing, but one eye could see the rapidly disappearing Irator. Garen yelled in frustration, trying to push, pull or roll the Brother away.

Irator was reaching out for the door handle, which Garen was dismayed to see had a lock on it. The Brother was very persistent. Garen finally resorted to violence, which took the Brother by surprise. The Brother whimpered and began to roll off. As the clothing cleared his face and he prepared to leap to his feet, the door swung open of it's own accord. Irator reflexively pulled his hand back, but too slowly. The door barrelled into him as a hairy brown shape pelted through the gap, followed by angry voices.

Sciel, complete with a battered loaf of bread, was halfway across the room before he noticed Garen. He was sitting on the floor, puzzled by the appearance of his friend, but fascinated by the events behind the door. Sciel turned to Garen then to Irator.

The Brother was holding the Soul jar reverently in his hands. He was staring at a long crack in the jar, which had appeared when the door handle had collided with it. Again the jar was vibrating, the crack growing with each pulse. A faint orange light began to shine from the crack, a haze gathered above the jar, growing, thickening, until it seemed a massive rain drop hung in the room. The drop hovered for a moment, rippling, billowing like a sail, then headed for the window.

The room was deathly silent, all attention focused on this strange event. The drop flattened against the glass noiselessly. It rolled, undulating like a fat, opaque maggot up and down the window. It found a crack in one of the small panes, flowed through it and was gone.

Raised voices once again sounded outside the door. Sciel, who was only mildly interested in something inedible, grabbed Garen's hand.

"We go quick, big trouble coming."

When Garen was too slow, Sciel yanked him to his feet and dragged him out of the room. The last Garen saw was a very distraught Irator, a Brother holding his ribs and several soldiers armed with nets running past the door.

He allowed himself to be lead until the sound of pursuit diminished.

"Sciel, stop, we have something to do."

Garen had decided he was going to smash all the jars, every single one. That's what they had come for originally, that's what they would do. Even if Kymar wasn't here, at least he had Sciel, who could break almost anything. Looking round for familiar sights, he oriented himself and headed for the narrow passage.

Chapter Nineteen

A long wagon creaked out of the market place towards the large gate. The back of the wagon contained sacks of flour, some fruit and a barrel of pickled chestnuts. In the driving seat was a short farmer with thick brown hair. He expertly steered the four oxen towards the open road. He had been told to take his load home and to take a young girl with him. She was to be looked after until she settled in, then paired off with one of his brothers. The man felt a vague contentment with this, it was time one of them had a child.

The girl sat beside the farmer silently. She had been told to go with this man, who would take care of her. Something made her uneasy, but every time she thought about it she couldn't quite penetrate the grey fog. She knew her name, and that she had a friend called Garen. She remembered many things, but there was no detail. Kymar looked down at her hand, that had detail. She could see the tiny lines and swirls on her fingertips. When she tried the same with her mind the fog was always there.

The cart rumbled across the cobbles under the gateway. One or two soldiers looked them over but said nothing. As the lead oxen emerged into sunlight the girl suddenly lurched forward in her seat. The man stopped the cart to see if the girl was well. She sat on the edge of her seat breathing deeply, her eyes wide. The man wondered if he should tell somebody, he hadn't seen many ill people.

Kymar was in a whirl. She had been sitting still, thinking about fog when suddenly a tiny whirlwind had entered her mind. It was fast and bright, it zipped around blowing away the fog.

It stopped blowing, growing brighter instead, until it lit her from within. Kymar was sure others could see the light as it charged out of every pore. She was elated, felt like dancing and singing, jumping for joy, running for the sheer pleasure of movement. Kymar's thoughts returned, her memories all stacking neatly into place. Her years of living in the forest snapped back. Finally, the events of the last few days clicked into place, she remembered where she was and why.

The young girl who seconds earlier had been almost lifeless, sprang from the cart like an acrobat. Kymar ran back towards the castle gate, a lightness in her step that hadn't been there before. One of the guards noticed her approach and shouted a warning. To Kymar the guard's speech and movement was unnaturally slow, as though he was underwater and she wasn't. She snatched a mace from the guard as he neared, knocked him senseless with it, then skipped into the castle before his comrades could even move.

She was on a high, Kymar knew, so let's not waste it she thought. Her mind was a swirling torrent of ideas. The return of part of her soul had ordered her mind, linking memories that were previously disjointed. It was as though someone had taken her fat lapdog and brought her back a sleek hunting hound. She also knew what she was going to do now. The thought of all those people living in perpetual fog. Generations of children unable to laugh or play, her anger rose.

She had worked out approximately where the Soul jars would be. Every conversation, every rumour, every scrap of information she had ever heard about the castle, about Soul jars, was now in one place. The pieces fit more or less exactly, rumour sifted from fact. The jars are at the top of the castle, in a secret chamber.

The only thing she wasn't sure of was what the souls would do when released. Some said they would die, she knew that to be untrue. Others that the souls had to be within a certain distance of the body they belonged to. What that distance was she didn't know. She had to try, not to would mean betraying all her mother had ever worked for, and that was unthinkable.

Her mind was alive as she threaded her way through the castle, the mace held ready before her. She had felt this feeling before, a feeling that she was moving at a faster rate than everybody else. Like the time in the forest when she had rescued Garen. The sword in her hand had felt light, her movements were graceful, almost balletic. In contrast the movements of the soldiers were slow and stilted. Now she felt that thrill all the time.

Kymar reached a set of stairs she had used to reach the kitchens. This time she went up, three steps at a time. On one of the landings a soldier swung the butt end of his spear at Kymar. Almost casually she ducked, barely a hand's width, but that was plenty and the spear went whistling over her head. She carried on up the stairs.

A few flights later, as she suspected the stairs ran out. Looking through a window she saw that there was indeed another floor. There was also someone on the roof, someone she knew.

The figure and several soldiers vanished from sight, seemingly melting into the roof. Kymar's newly arranged mind fitted facts together in a split second. If the soldiers were on guard duty then Parsathan wouldn't have been there. If there was no threat already present the soldiers would be down here, not giving away secrets by tramping across roofs. The only threat she knew of to the Soul jars was her or Garen. Therefore Garen must already be there.

Looking out of the window she spotted a drain spout that appeared climbable. She set off around the building towards the nearest window. The window was easily opened, unfortunately two soldiers spotted her and came running down the corridor.

To Kymar the soldiers looked comical, bouncing at her in slow motion. One was slightly quicker than the other and reached her half a step ahead. He had obviously been ordered to capture her alive as he swung a wooden club not his sword. Kymar leaned back and watched the club waft past her nose, as it carried on round she brought the mace sharp against his elbow, with a backhanded strike. The sharp flange of the maze crunched against bone, knocking his arm around into the path of the other soldier. The club hit the second soldier's arm ruining his concentration. He tried to recover, but as he looked round the mace impacted with his metal rimmed helm turning his knees to jelly. He started to go down. Kymar then swiped the first soldier with a forehanded attack. His helm took some of the force but he was already off balance, he fell sideways in a daze. All the action had taken place in only a few seconds, to Kymar it was plenty of time.

She returned her attention to the window, opening it and climbing onto the sill. The climb was easier than she thought. It made her think of Sciel, he would probably have managed it with his eyes shut and a large snack in his hand.

Up on the flat roof she quickly moved to where she had seen Parsathan and his cronies disappear. Sure enough there was a set of steps leading down into a long room. The folding steps had been covered over by a thick piece of grey painted wood. It would have been very difficult to spot if it hadn't been open.

Inside she could hear raised voices, someone shouting then someone talking loudly. She leapt down the steps, landing with barely a sound. A faint click sounded under her foot as she landed. She stayed crouched as behind her the stairs slowly lifted back into the roof. Kymar let the stairs rise, she would have plenty of time to find a way out when the deed was done.

She looked around at all the shelves of jars, it was difficult even for her boosted mind to grasp the sheer numbers of Soul jars that were located here. Kymar studied one or two of them before moving on.

Around a corner up ahead she could see the shadow of one of the soldiers. The shouting, definitely Garen's, was coming from that direction. She sneaked up to the corner then peered around it. Her face was only a few feet from the nearest soldier, but he remained unaware of her presence. Parsathan and Irator were standing ten paces ahead of the group of soldiers talking into what looked like an alcove. Parsathan's voice was loud, but not shouting. Garen's reply came shouting back from the alcove. Irator was making suggestions in a low voice. Parsathan was obviously trying to convert Garen to his cause. So far Garen was resisting.

Kymar was sure she could beat all six of the soldiers, but not all at once. She was sure Garen would join in, that still left seven to two. Unless Sciel was there, she hadn't heard him yet but that wasn't unusual. Kymar didn't like to admit it but she would sooner have had Sciel on her side than Garen.

Well she thought, there was no other choice, we came here to free the souls, that's what I'm going to do. Either we do the job or I go to see mother.

Kymar sneaked back along the room until she was as far from Parsathan as she could be. Then she picked a shelf and began smashing. The mace swung again and again, not in a frenzy, but in a controlled hurry. Soul jars scattered in all directions, some of them smashed, some of them cracked, some of them didn't break at all.

Garen was backed into a corner near the screen. Sciel was hanging half in half out of the hole. They had found the room after a long search, then climbed into the Soul jar chamber through the hole he had made earlier. But Parsathan had been waiting, he should have known he would be. The soldiers he came across during the search had ignored him.

Now the room below was occupied by soldiers, all holding wooden clubs ringed with iron. He had expected Parsathan to have him carted away, but he just stood there talking, trying to convince him of the rightness of his ways. Garen had become annoyed, had started shouting back, about Kymar and his father, about the lives of the people he knew.

"…Think of all the benefits of our society, Garen. I know I've said it before, but it does make sense. No crime, no hunger, no suffering, widows and orphans looked after, everyone given a worthwhile job to do. What else could we do? What other methods could we use to create such an ordered society?"

"Anything!" Garen yelled, "Anything but this, ripping part of someone's soul out is not right, no matter what the result. People should be free to do as they please, not be told every move they make. There must be another way, I don't know what it is but it's not this…"

The silence that had fallen was disturbed by a violent crashing. Three of the soldiers turned and ran in the direction of the sound. Parsathan turned and followed after, Irator too, but moving a little faster, the other three soldiers stayed put. Garen listened but could only hear the smashing. He turned to Sciel, a question in his expression.

"Your female, smashing jars, many jars." Whispered Sciel after sniffing and listening.

Garen was jubilant, her soul had returned, it does work. Then he was suddenly afraid, three soldiers had gone after her. He was an easy going person usually, he knew Kymar was a natural when it came to hitting people, but he wasn't. He didn't like all this violence. But there was a difference between liking and doing when necessary. He looked at Sciel, flicked his eyes to the right then suddenly ran.

The three remaining soldiers were more interested in the action around the corner than Garen, so were unable to stop him as he dashed by. Garen ran along the room, through the box, behind the dummy and waited for the first soldier. Sciel had started last but was already in the small room when Garen got there.

When the soldier appeared in the box Garen and Sciel pushed with all their might sending the dummy soldier crashing into the real one. They knew it wouldn't hold them for long but it was better than nothing. They dashed through the other side and around to where Kymar was making a stand.

Orange light glowed all around, massive raindrops shimmered and pulsed against the windows. This part of the room was noticeably warmer than the rest. Many hundred jars lay scattered and broken. Many thousands remained intact.

Parsathan had ordered the soldiers not to break any of the jars. As they were scattered all over the floor this made the assault particularly difficult. Every time the soldiers approached Kymar she backed off and spread more jars over the floor with her mace. Garen was amazed, she was wielding the mace with the same skill as she had used with the sword, he was certain she hadn't used either until a few weeks ago. He ran up to her and began pulling jars off the shelves and throwing them on the floor.

"No, at the soldiers, throw them at the soldiers!" Shouted Kymar. She didn't sound at all surprised to see me thought Garen. Women, I'll never understand them.

He picked up a jar and threw it at the nearest soldier. Sciel quickly got the message and did the same. Garen's jars missed more often but landed harder. Sciel seldom missed, but his didn't impact with such force.

At first the soldiers braved the onslaught, one of them getting close enough to take a swipe at Kymar. She deftly knocked the club from his hand, then sent him sprawling on his back with a well placed blow. The other soldiers joined in from the other side but were similarly hampered, by flying jars and jar filled floors. Parsathan stood back, a look of total dismay on his face. All those souls free. All that anarchy and chaos, those poor children just didn't understand.

Parsathan turned to Irator, "Assemble the Brothers, tell them to bring all the Soul jars they can find. And give Krane a message. Tell her to bring the archers."

"The archers Brother? Surely not!" argued Irator.

"I have had enough of this Brother Irator. We cannot have all those people burdened again."

"But what about your successor?"

"Brother Irator, please, deliver the message!"

Irator turned slowly, then walked away mumbling under his breath.

The room was filling up with souls now, the big raindrops floated everywhere. It seemed the windows were sealed tight, there were no doors either in this part of the room. The air was thick with souls as more and more jars were broken. Garen was having particular problems, as the souls he freed seem to hover around him. He had already gathered quite a mass of them, at times only his legs remained visible. Garen aimed for a target, but as he threw the jar a soul drifted before the projectile. The jar flew into the soul, halved its speed and emerged at a different angle, completely missing the soldier it was aimed at.

These things are getting in the way, he thought.

The sound of booted feet marching came closer and closer. From both directions soldiers appeared, fully armed with swords and shields, not guards with soft armour and clubs.

"Garen, Sciel come here, stand back to back, if we get split up we're lost. Gather as many jars as you can, at least we can release a few more before we go."

Garen didn't like the sound of that, why don't we just surrender he thought. But he didn't say it.

They stood back to back against one wall. The souls that had been attracted to Garen now floated and whirled around all three of them. For a moment Garen thought they could hide behind them, but they were too spread out.

The soldiers in front of Garen suddenly withdrew until he could see only their shadows just around the corner. He called out to Kymar, "Something is wrong, the soldiers have pulled back."

"Yes I think I know why. There are archers at this end."

"What?" Garen yelled, turning to look. As he shouted the souls around him vibrated, producing a wave of heat. Garen tried to look at the archers but there were too many souls in the way. "I wish these things would move so I can see what's happening," he shouted impatiently. To his amazement the souls drifted to one side as though a breeze had wafted them. The archers were crouched behind the soldiers with shields, stringing their bows.

Kymar looked at Garen, "How did you do that? Quick put them back."

The archers pulled arrows from quivers.

"Go back, back to where you were." said Garen loudly. The souls didn't move.

"What's wrong? Try again, come on!" cried Kymar.

The archers nocked their arrows, and prepared to fire.

"Don't rush me," screamed Garen. The souls vibrated.

The archers looked to Parsathan for the signal.

"That's it!" yelled Garen in triumph. "Emotion, they respond to emotion!" The souls vibrated almost audibly in response.

Garen looked towards Parsathan, the priest's mouth began to open.

"Come to me!" he yelled with as much feeling as he could muster.

"Fire at will," said Parsathan softly, reluctantly, then he turned away, head bowed.

Garen's eyes focused on the points of the arrows, they all receded backwards as the archers drew their bows. The souls were moving towards him, but slowly too slowly. "Come to me now!" he screamed with all the fear and panic he could project.

The bubbles of heat haze flowed towards Garen, every soul in the room moved towards the brilliant light of his emotion. The view of the soldiers shimmered, distorted as more and more souls crowded together. But the sound came through clear, a snapping, cracking sound as strings slapped the backs of bows, propelling iron tipped shafts into the fume.

The arrows flew true through the first soul, into the second, into the third. Then slowed, slowed again, changing course as they tried to penetrate the mass. Finally, all momentum spent, the arrows dropped one by one to the floor.

"Well, that seems to have worked." Garen grinned.

"But what do we do now? We can't go home like this."

A sudden yell made them all tense. At the end of the room captain Krane was pushing through the archers. "Charge!" she shouted, "Come on form up behind me."

Some of the soldiers formed up in a square of nine, shields and swords at the ready. Krane was already into the haze, it was an insubstantial barrier to solid matter.

Kymar was ready for Krane, with her mind working so fast it really looked like Krane was running through jelly. The nine soldiers approached the haze, and would have hesitated if their captain hadn't already been in it. Kymar knew they didn't stand much chance against this many.

"Better think of something fast, Garen or we will all be joining this lot." She gestured towards the souls with her mace.

For some reason Garen thought of his father. Would he be disappointed when he found out? Would anyone even tell him? Did he have enough soul left to be sad. The thought of sadness flooded Garen's brain, his shoulders slumped. He grabbed Sciel by the arm, "Sorry friend," he whispered.

Krane raised her sword as she leapt towards Kymar, who stood ready with the mace. But the blow never came. Kymar was astonished to see a tear roll down the captain's cheek. The nine soldiers had also stopped, turning away from each other in embarrassment.

Kymar reached out and touched one of the souls. She was immediately gripped by a sudden grief, as though her mother had died that very instant. "Garen, what are you doing?" A warm tear rolled down her face. She snatched her finger back.

"What?" said Garen confused, "What's happening?" He looked around, his mouth hanging open, "What have I done?"

"I don't know, but whatever it is don't stop yet. I need to think."

The soldiers outside the haze shuffled nervously from foot to foot. The archers lowered their bows, unsure what to make of this strange site, grown men, hardened fighters, crying? They looked around for a leader. Parsathan had left, their captain was standing crying like a babe. What now?

A loud chanting filled the room. Brothers began to appear at the other end of the room, more followed, all chanting, all carrying Soul Jars. That end of the room was suddenly filled with Brothers, some wearing hospital uniforms, others in bed wear, most in their white and red habits.

"Garen, we have to do something quick before the souls are put back in the jars."

"Break a window, let them all out!" shouted Garen.

Sciel leapt towards a window, breaking things was something he understood.

"No! Not yet, we have to release all the souls first. Without protection we won't be able to. Garen, smash a jar, but think about it whilst you do it."

"I do think about it don't I? Oh, I see what you mean."

Garen picked up a jar and looked at it. He hated that jar, hated it more than life itself, he wanted to break it, smash it into a thousand pieces, to free the soul inside. It was a true feeling so he was able to project it into the souls. The souls transmitted it into the soldiers. They straightened, dried their eyes and began to look around. One by one the soldiers, including Krane, began picking up jars and smashing them to the ground. Being soldiers they were very good at this.

The men outside the haze took one look then ran for help.

The chanting battled with the smashing of jars to fill the room. More and more souls crammed into the space, each trying to come near Garen. The haze extended down the room in both directions, the Brothers unable to keep up with the relentless crashing and cracking of jars.

The outer edge of the haze reached the first line of Brothers. By now the emotion of jar breaking was pulsing through the haze, so that anyone merely touching the souls was swept into action. The Brothers fought as long as they could against the urge, but were finally overcome by sheer numbers.

After what seemed like only minutes every jar in the room had been smashed. But the emotion was so strong some of the soldiers continued, smashing the broken jars into fragments.

Garen stopped, then began to think calm relaxed thoughts.

After a while the whole room fell quite. Garen couldn't see more than a few feet through the thick haze. It was very hot, the room was stifling.

"What now?" whispered Kymar, "If we let all these go how do we get out?"

"Perhaps I can get them to follow us for a while, then send them off home."

"It's worth a try, come on, we can use the steps up to the roof."

"I knew there had to be another way in, I never found it though, I just made my own."

The three friends walked around the room until Kymar stopped them, "They are here somewhere, it's just a matter of finding them."

Sciel ran to the wall and began to dig his long fingers into every crack and gap. After only a few moments there was a loud click and the ceiling began to drop down. As soon as light appeared through the crack the heat haze began to flow out of it.

The gap widened, a great surge of souls rushed through. The pressure and temperature in the room immediately abated.

To Garen's delight many of the souls stayed with him, circling around him like tame birds. Out on the roof the heat haze could be seen as an elongating ribbon, soaring into the sky.

They stood for a moment, enraptured by the sight, the deed of what they had achieved. Sciel searched the rooftops for a way out, one humans could manage, which wasn't easy.

"Come, Garen, I hungry, we go eat now, climb down pipe and go home."

The ribbon headed off towards the mountains, melting into the distance. "Yes, let's get away while we can, then we can send the rest of these souls back to where they came from."

After climbing across various rooftops, each lower than the other, they found themselves on a green field outside the kitchens. They were soon back down the hill the castle stood and on heading for home. Inside the castle they could hear the sounds of shouting, soldiers being given orders, servants refusing them. And the sound of gates being locked, windows shuttered.

"Sounds like they're expecting company," Kymar said.

"I think they'll get it as well, I wonder how long it will take?"

"Perhaps you ought to send the rest of the souls away now, they may be able to catch up to the others."

Garen stood quietly for a moment, his eyes closed. His breathing slowed, his head tipped forward. After a few minutes the souls began to drift away in ones and twos until only one remained.

He slowly opened one eye to check if they had gone. Garen looked at the one remaining soul with a puzzled look on his face. Suddenly his eyes widened and he smiled. "Come on, let's go," he called and began to walk down the hill.

"But what about that one? You can't just keep it," cried Kymar.

"It's alright," said Garen without turning, "I'll deliver this one personally."

The End

Details

Date

22nd-24th Sept 2006

Venue

Britannia Hotel, Nottingham

Guests Of Honour

Clive Barker, Raymond Feist, Neil Gaiman,
Ramsey Campbell and Juliet E. McKenna

Master of Ceremonies

David J. Howe

www.fantasycon.org.uk